They'll warm your heart and tickle your fancy; they'll steal into your life before you even realize what has happened!

Such is the power of the exceptional family that has made Thyra Ferré Bjorn into a best-selling author besieged by fans who demand encore after encore.

First came PAPA'S WIFE, then PAPA'S DAUGHTER and MAMA'S WAY; now DEAR PAPA, a heartwarming chronicle of a lively, loving family as remembered by Mama herself, now at the end of a long and full life.

Do you care enough to love the very best? If so, DEAR PAPA is for you!

DEAR PAPA

Thyra Ferré Bjorn

PILLAR BOOKS NEW YORK

DEAR PAPA

A PILLAR BOOK
Published by arrangement with Holt, Rinehart and Winston

Pillar Books edition published April 1976

ISBN: 0-89129-138-5

Copyright © 1963 by Thyra Ferré Bjorn

Printed in the United States of America

PILLAR BOOKS
(Harcourt Brace Jovanovich)
757 Third Avenue, New York, New York 10017, U.S.A.

To my dear sisters,
Margaret,
Ann,
Karin,
this book is
affectionately dedicated.

A Word
to the Reader

Sometimes it happens that an author is forced to write a book she loves writing and *Dear Papa* is such a book. Almost every day letters pour in to my home here in Longmeadow asking me so many questions about Mama. Is she still living? Is she well? What happened to all the children? Where are they living?

Some of these are personal questions which I must not answer. My family likes privacy and not one of them wants to be looked upon as a character in a book, although they all do appreciate the great interest in the Franzon family. But I, who started it all, have to protect them wherever I can. So I knew I would write one last book about the Franzons, telling all there is to tell. This is especially fitting at this time when the deep pain of Mama's graduation from earthlife still lingers as a dull ache in my heart.

When I write, I like to have freedom. Although my stories are based on fact, I don't want any readers to take them too literally. I have a vivid imagination and I love letting it play wherever it wants to.

So now I begin my fourth book by writing in the same vein as *Papa's Wife* and *Papa's Daughter*. I take so much fact and so much fiction and mix them long and carefully together in imagination's big mixing bowl, until I myself cannot tell one from the other.

Please read my book just for the pleasure of it and I hope it will give you a joyous, worth-while reading experience.

Sincerely,
Thyra Ferré Bjorn

Longmeadow, Massachusetts

Prologue

It was about the turn of the century when lovely, young Maria Skogberg tramped up the path to the red and white parsonage in Swedish Lapland to apply for a job as maid for the bachelor minister who lived alone in the big house. Pastor Franzon hired her despite the fact that she was only sixteen. But he did not know that becoming his maid was, in Maria's calculation, only a prelude to becoming his lovely wife and one day reigning as mistress of the parsonage. Yes, that young girl had great ambitions and she started laying the ground-work for their realization the minute Pastor Franzon gave the word that she could have the job. She began by cooking the best food a man had ever tasted and doing it so economically that it cost only half of what his other maids had spent. And she kept his house orderly, giving it those little touches that only a woman's hand can create. Her laughter and smile filled the whole parsonage with a warmth and gaiety the pastor had never dreamed could exist there.

There was only one cloud in Mama's blue sky. Pontus Franzon was not the least bit romantic. He didn't even seem to notice the little tricks a woman uses to catch her man. And the years went on with the pastor overjoyed at the way his household was kept and the cheerfulness that shone over it, but having no intention whatsoever of proposing to Maria.

After four years Maria took fate into her own small hands. She left the parsonage and went to America. Pastor Franzon had been willing to let her go because he did not want to stand in the way of all that America could offer a young girl. Of course, he did not realize that this was Maria's last desperate attempt to get him to understand that he was in love, although he hadn't discovered it yet himself.

In America, Maria found a job as second cook with a very fine old family, related to the Vanderbilts, who had a mansion on Fifth Avenue in New York City. Maria found a wonderfully exciting life in her new country, but her love for Pontus Franzon did not fade. One day she wrote him a letter and marked her address plainly. Then she waited. It took months before the hoped-for answer finally arrived. Pastor Franzon missed her very much. He could not find a satisfactory maid and he pleaded with her to come back to her old job. Maria was furious. She had never been so furious in all her life. The nerve of him, asking her to leave all the glory of this new "promised land" to come back and slave for him. But after she simmered down, she made one last attempt to make him understand. In her short, sweet letter she stated her requirements for returning . . . never as his maid . . . but if he had a better offer, to let her know. She had been very bold, but no answer came from Lapland. The months went by and Maria was beginning to give up her dream of becoming Mrs. Franzon and turn her attention to new clothes and the young man who was the butler where she worked. Then suddenly, as unexpected as lightning in a clear blue sky, Pastor Franzon came to America.

As Maria was walking in Central Park on her afternoon off whom should she see sitting on a park bench but Pastor Franzon. She believed then that he had really come to fetch her home as his bride, but he still had no such thoughts. All he wanted was for her to return as his housekeeper with the promise that he would never fire her. She could make it her life job. It was then that Maria threw away all her pride and spoke to him in no uncertain terms. The only way she would return with him was as Mrs. Franzon. He just couldn't believe his ears. But Maria did not give in and so Pastor Franzon decided that perhaps he would have to pay the price of his freedom for a super housekeeper. She was young and beautiful, full of life, strong and able to work. So he said, "yes," and Maria was dancing on clouds. She had won! She would be his wife in a few days, quit her job, and return to dear old Lapland. But on the wedding day, when they both stood solemnly before the preacher to say those binding sacred words, Pastor Franzon suddenly began to panic at the thought of losing his freedom. And when the preacher asked him, "Do you take this woman to be your lawful, wedded wife?", he answered, "No, I'd better not!"

As they came out of the preacher's home, Maria walked away from Pontus Franzon after telling him just what she thought of him. She looked so proud and beautiful and undaunted as she turned her back on him that for the first time in his life he felt completely helpless, lonely, and unhappy. She had never been more beautiful and he had been a fool. Who would look after him in his old age? Who would laugh with him and love him? The only one who qualified for that job was Maria. He waited a whole night, not sleeping, just thinking and getting rid of his fear of becoming a married man. In the wee hours of the morning, he knew that he loved Maria, but he had to wait until morning to call and tell her so. She was not too overjoyed at his late proposal. She was still hurt and humiliated, but he used his best preaching techniques and talked her into returning to him, which she finally did because love is like that. This time they were married and, two days later, boarded the ship for Sweden. Then Maria Franzon got her first big disappointment. She was on her honeymoon, but since Pastor Franzon had had his stateroom all taken care of, his bride had to share one with a schoolteacher. It was a sorrowful beginning, a honeymoon minus the honey. But Maria tried to take it and she promised herself that she would teach Pontus Franzon what love was. It took a while after they came back to the parsonage, for the surprised church members had had no idea that their pastor had married . . . and his former maid, half his age, at that. But they all loved Maria and soon she was a favorite among them with her tender loving ways and her gaiety and helpfulness. Yes, Pastor Franzon was a lucky man to have a wife like Maria who would be such a charming helpmate through the years ahead.

Then the family began to come . . . first a redhead (and poor Papa hated red hair); second a crybaby; then came the angel, after Mama bought a picture of one to have as a model for her future children. The Franzons finally had eight children, which Mama claimed was a safe number and Papa declared was a lucky one.

It was Mama who wanted the family to move to America. She had never forgotten that wonderful country across the ocean where she had spent just one year. It was the only land where her family could get an education and all the opportunities to become great men and women. So she talked Papa into resigning his pastorate in Lapland and leaving the little white church to move to the new land where a Swedish-speaking congregation was waiting for him.

What a thrill it was for the youngsters to see New York, even though two of them did get lost on a subway and the pastor's family was missing from the reception waiting for them in Berkley Hills. But the boys were found and the whole family began their new life.

Their parsonage was furnished with a conglomeration of cast-off furniture donated by the church members, but little by little they acquired a few new things. After a few years, Papa's nerves became strained and he took a two-year leave of absence from his church and bought a little farm. The farm years were sunny ones for the Franzons. Papa became a well man and returned to his preaching. The children began to grow up and many things happened to the family.

Then one day Papa and Mama returned to their homeland for a visit. They had the most magnificent time together until Midsummer Day when they were climbing Gellivara mountain, and Papa's heart gave out. He could not reach the top with Mama. . . . She had to leave Papa to sleep his last sleep in Sweden, his own beloved country. Her grief was deep and hard, but she returned to America with strength and courage, tears in her eyes, but a smile on her lips. All of them missed Papa terribly, but the children had their own lives to live and news of a first grandchild brought a ray of sunshine into Mama's sorrow.

After Kerstin, the youngest, was married, Mama moved to Miami, Florida, where she bought a little white bungalow, thus carrying out the plans she and Papa had had for their old age. Nim had become a surgeon there, so she had one of her children near her. . . .

So the years go by, and Mama reaches the age of eighty-one. She knows that soon she is going to be with Papa. She has lived a triumphant life and death holds no terror for her. The story goes on from here as Mama writes a letter to Papa, sharing many things about their eight children and telling of the longing in her heart to be with him.

Chapter One

It was a beautiful garden and Mama loved it very much. It was neither too large nor too small, but just right. Even the roses had taken root and begun to bloom. It had taken a long time before Mr. Gale, the man who worked out of doors for Mama, had found the right place for them. Now sometimes, when the wind blew in the right direction, the perfume from those roses drifted in through the kitchen screen door and filled the whole house with their lovely scent. It always made Mama homesick for New England, for the parsonage in Berkley Hills, where each year, in the latter part of May and the beginning of June, the roses had been extraordinarily beautiful. Back in those days she had picked a bouquet of them daily and placed it in the big vase in the living room. Papa had not been pleased at that. Mama smiled, remembering how he would stare at them for a moment, then storm at her, making his voice very gruff.

"Maria, you have picked some of those roses again."

But Mama had only smiled her sweetest smile. "And that is why they grow so well, darling," she had said. "Roses thrive on giving and sharing their loveliness. The more you take of their bloom, the lovelier and more abundant they become. It's their way of giving thanks for such good care."

A few years after Papa's death, Mama, as Mrs. Maria

15

Franzon, had moved from New England to make her home in Miami, Florida. She hadn't been able to grow roses in her garden by the little white bungalow, although everything else had bloomed in great profusion. But Mr. Gale had finally found the right spot for them and Mama was thrilled over her rose bed.

Each evening, after the supper dishes were done, Mama would go out into her garden, where she stretched out in the comfortable lounging chair her oldest son, Dr. Nim, had given her as a special gift. She called this her "sunset tryst" and to her it was the dearest hour of the day. It was a time of reminiscence, when she could turn her thoughts back into the past. Those pages of yesteryears, as she turned them in her book of memories night after night, seemed to pile up until now they had become a volume.

Mama smiled to herself as she thought of the dishes. There were not very many now, although she still prepared a big dinner for herself each night. Her love for cooking had never left her. But *one* at the dinner table did not amount to much! Mama's heart warmed as she remembered the parsonage in Lapland, Sweden, when Papa had had a small church and there had been eight children to feed. How she used to cook for them! And the pile of dishes had been stacked high. After they had moved to America, there had been another parsonage. And as the children grew, it had seemed to Mama that there was no end to their appetites. They were always so hungry. And Papa himself—bless his memory—had had a good appetite.

How many years was it since he had left her? It was way back in 1938. She had not believed in that dark beginning that the years could have moved on without him. But they had, and now she was an old lady. And that daily pile of dishes had grown smaller and smaller as the years rolled by and the children had left home for college or marriage. The last one to leave had been her baby, Kerstin. After she had married Jim, Mama had moved to Miami.

16

This was a cozy house, with a wide porch. It had four good-sized rooms and all the furniture had been bought new. She had felt a little like a bride moving into this home. She had never had the pleasure of living in a home with new furniture before. Papa's bachelor parsonage had been furnished long before he had met her. Even in America, the parsonage had already been furnished by kind church members and everything had been there for them to use when they arrived. Later, when some of the furniture had been returned upon the request of the owners, Papa had bought some new pieces to replace them. But the result had been a funny conglomeration, a mixture of old and new. In this house, however, everything had been brand-new. Every piece had been picked out by Mama, herself, and put in its right place. It had been such a joy shopping for her little home. But even that seemed far away now. The only things she had saved from their old home were gifts given to the Franzons by church groups on special occasions—and her dishes. The first were keepsakes she would never part with and the dishes were even more precious. She would never part with them, no matter how old they were. And how handy it had been to have enough plates and things when the children came to visit with their families on vacations. Sometimes it had seemed as though the walls would burst because there were so many grandchildren, and now even great grandchildren. That was the blessing of growing old, Mama was thinking, to see the new generation beginning where the old left off.

Greta was the only one of her eight children who had never married. But Papa would have been very proud of Greta, for she had set education even ahead of a husband. Greta, a college professor, was just getting her doctorate degree. She had been working towards it for seven years, and she claimed that those busy years had given her no time for romance. Mama silently wondered about it though. There had been a beautiful romance once in Greta's life. Was this daugh-

17

ter of hers one of those people who loved only once, who could never forget a broken romance? Or was Greta waiting for time to heal and mend? Mama did not know and she would never ask because that would seem like prying. Only time would tell. But her Greta would have made such a fine wife and mother, and what a good cook and housekeeper! Mama could not imagine that anything in the world could be more important and wonderful than being married.

Tonight Mama was pondering a dream she had had a couple of nights ago. It was a strange dream and so real that she couldn't get it out of her mind. But it was a dear dream and she was glad it had come to her. Now she wondered if it had a special meaning. Was Pontus calling her to come to him? She would not mind. She had lived a long, full life, crowded with love and joy and happiness. In her heart she was still young. She still felt the same eagerness to begin each day and that bubbling-over feeling of gladness when letters arrived from her children. How fast her heart beat when Nim's big car stopped outside her home each morning, and she heard the footsteps of her son, the doctor, coming up her walk. Nim was a dear son. Even though he was a busy surgeon, he took time to drop in to see her each day. Mama had a feeling that Nim had been especially prompt about these morning calls since her heart attack two years ago.

It had happened the day before Christmas Eve, just when Vickey and John and their three children had arrived for the holidays. Instead of preparing a big smorgasbord for Christmas Eve, she had been put to bed. She had been so near to crossing the dark river. Nim had insisted that she should go to the hospital and it had been his strong will against hers, as he stood there with two other doctors.

"You see, Nim," she had said, trying to give power to her weak voice, "I will go to Heaven anytime, but never to the hospital."

And she had won out. She had stayed in her own

home with Vickey to care for her. And when Vickey had to leave, a practical nurse had come to stay with her. Nim had looked troubled at times when he examined her. And then, as the children began to come, one by one, from far and wide, to visit her, Mama understood that her illness was more serious than she had realized. The last two children to arrive had been Button and Greta. They had driven down from the East to spend three weeks with her.

Button had sent the nurse home. "Greta and I will take over now, Mama," she had said.

And Mama had been glad because she loved to be cared for by her girls.

Then one morning a new attack had seized her. She had tried to hide the effects of it at first, but Greta had taken one long look at her and started for the phone to call Nim. But Mama had been able to make her voice heard.

"No, my dear," she had said, shaking her head, "don't call your brother. He might want me to go to the hospital and I am not going. If my time is up, I want to die here in my own little home with you two girls beside me. You have to listen to me. This is my wish."

Greta had placed the telephone receiver back on the hook, glancing at Button. Button had nodded and Mama knew that the girls would respect her wish.

Later on that day she had been sure she was facing her last hours in this world. She began to reckon the time since she had felt the weakness coming over her. It had taken her own mother six hours to die, and six hours for her mother's mother. She had about four more hours, she had calculated. Gently she had told the girls about it and had been surprised to see the horror written on their faces.

"Dying is not anything to be afraid of," she had told them as they sat beside her bed taking turns holding her hand. "It's just an experience, like being born, or growing out of childhood. It's just as much a part of life, and fear is not going to alter it."

19

They had sat there beside her as the hours had ticked away. Once Mama had tried to drink a little tea, but found it too hard to swallow. It would be strange and empty for her children not to have Mama. She had always been such a part of them. They would be filled with loneliness, knowing that she wasn't there to turn to. Perhaps she was selfish to want to go like this. She felt sorriest for Greta, who had no husband. All the rest had their own growing families.

"Greta," Mama had whispered faintly, "why don't you pack my silver service? The one I brought from Sweden. I want you to take it now, while I am still here, so the others will know I gave it to you."

"Oh, Mama, don't talk like that, please," Greta sobbed. "You're not leaving us. You'll be better soon."

A little later, after Mama had closed her eyes and was dozing off, she had heard the girls talking between themselves. It was Button's whisper that had reached her ear.

"What shall we do, Greta?" she had heard Button say. "You know Mama is really dramatizing her own death. She's really planning to die in another hour."

It had pleased Mama to know that even in her helplessness she had the upper hand. But the girls had looked very sad and from time to time she saw them wipe their tears away. Lying there, so small and weak and helpless, Mama had closed her eyes and tried to catch a glimpse of eternity; but there was only darkness around her. This would have been such a beautiful way to go and she had wished the girls would understand that. But perhaps it was a selfish way. They still wanted her so much; she was breaking their hearts. She couldn't do it to them. I must get strength to get better, she had thought for the first time. I mustn't let it happen now. Strength had begun to come back and Mama had opened her eyes. Pulling together all the power she could, she had sat up in bed.

"Button and Greta," she had said, forcing a smile, "I have decided not to die. It isn't fair to leave you all

20

without a mother. You still need me. I will stay. What have you planned for dinner?"

Button had stared at her. "Dinner?" she cried. "How do you think we could think of dinner with you leaving us?"

"Well, wipe your tears away, darlings, and go and see what there is to eat because I am getting up and you are not going to stop me."

To the amazement of her daughters, Mama had left her bed, dressed with their help, and had sat at the dinner table that night forcing food into her mouth.

When Nim dropped in the next morning, he had smiled cheerfully. "Mama," he said, "your heart is much stronger. I predict you will live till you are one hundred years old."

Neither Button nor Greta had dared to tell Nim about the events of the day before.

Yes, Mama had been feeling very well ever since, every day sensing more strength returning. And two whole years had passed without a thought of leaving this world—until tonight. It was that strange dream that came to her mind time and time again.

In her dream Mama had been out in the woods picking blueberries. It must have been a Swedish woods because the fir trees were so tall and straight and there were so many white birches. And the berry bushes— well, they were all low bushes; they did not have high-bush blueberries in Sweden. Wherever she looked, it had been just blue with berries.

Mama had had a big pail that she was filling. When she came to an opening among the trees where she could see quite far off, her eyes suddenly opened wide because way over there, in another clearing, she saw Pontus. Yes, it was Papa picking berries, too. And as he straightened up, he caught sight of her and his face broke into a happy smile.

"Maria," he called as he waved at her, "come over here!"

Mama had looked at all the berries around her and at her pail, only half full.

"I can't, Pontus," she had cried. "There are too many berries here for me to pick."

"But, Maria, they are so much bigger here. Come on," his voice urged, strong and clear.

But Mama still hesitated. There were so many brambles and so much underbrush to walk through and there were all those berries she would have to leave unpicked.

But Papa kept waving and calling. "You have never seen berries like these over here, Maria. You just come and see."

She had begun to walk toward him then. Somehow she had not minded that the underbrush scratched her legs and that she had almost fallen several times. She had lifted her pail high and Papa had stood there smiling and waiting. When she was almost there, he had reached out his strong hand and helped her, taking her pail in his other hand.

"It is good that you came," he had said.

Then Mama had looked about and her eyes had opened wider and wider. "Why, Pontus," she had whispered, "I never dreamed that blueberries could be this big. And there are so many of them. The pail will be full in no time."

Papa had put his arms around her. "I am so glad you came, Maria. I told you you had never seen berries like these."

And then she had awakened and had not been able to go back to sleep again. "I never even had time to pick one of those big berries," she had said aloud. "It would have been so much fun to go on dreaming."

She knew she had spoken out loud to herself in the middle of the night. But it had been so good to see Pontus, and the rest of the night she had thought of him and wondered if soon now she would go to where he was waiting for her.

Mama stretched in her chair. The sun was sinking

22

fast now—darkness came so abruptly here in the southland—but it was glorious and golden between the tall palms whose finger leaves spread out in the twilight. The evening was balmy. It had been a hot day, but a tiny breeze from the bay made the evening very comfortable. April was a hot month and it brought a sun that would burn hotter and hotter from now until October.

As much as she loved the Florida winters, she had begun to dislike the heat of the summer months. These Southern summers were too hot for her to take, so in the latter part of June she would go to visit the children in New England. Button and Eric still lived in Berkley Hills, and Pelle and Felicia right outside of Boston. Torkel was a pastor in a church near Rochester, New York, and Greta was in Philadelphia, Pennsylvania. She would try to see them all this summer.

She smiled to herself. The children always made a fuss over whom she would visit first. What a blessed mother she was and how dear were her children. How lovingly and tenderly they cared for her. She was eighty-one years old on her last birthday. That *was* being old and she did look old. Her face in the mirror told her that very plainly. Her eyes were big and blue, and they looked back at her with a bit of mischief dancing in them. But there were wrinkles and deep lines, some like a crossword puzzle across her cheeks.

I don't mind them, she told herself, because they speak of character and long years of life. They tell the story of problems I have faced. It's life's pattern that has marked me. No one escapes sorrow and burdens and even when they don't come to you personally, you bear them for your children. Yes, she had spent many days trying to help her dear ones and many, many hours on her knees in prayer for them. But the joy had overshadowed the dark days and she would never fuss about those wrinkles. They were just part of growing old gracefully.

I wish I could tell Pontus all the things that have

happened since he left me, Mama was thinking as darkness descended on her little garden. I wish he could have seen my little home here and shared it with me. It had been their dream since they came to America that when Papa was too old to have a church, they would move to Florida. That was why Mama had carried it out. And since Nim and Karin had settled in Miami, it had been easy for her to decide to move there, too.

Tonight Mama was lonesome for Papa, for the old life they used to share. He had left her much too soon and there was no tangible way to keep in touch with him, although she knew in her heart that his spirit was always close to her. Never before, not even in those first dark hours when Papa had left her, had she had such a strong desire to communicate with him. If this was a premonition, then she, too, would soon leave this earth.

Presently a thought entered her mind. Why couldn't she write him a letter? Even if her letter could not be mailed to him, why couldn't she talk to him on paper, making believe it would reach him somewhere? It would give her deep satisfaction and perhaps take the edge off this strange loneliness she was feeling. She *would* write Pontus a letter. It would be a long, long letter, like a story. It would take up much of her time and would give her a mission to fulfill. And when she had departed from this world, one of the children would find it and know that she had known she soon would leave.

I won't plan what to write, she thought, but just let it form its own pattern. But it must be gay and real and wonderful.

"Tomorrow I'll begin to write to Pontus," she said out loud as she left the garden and walked toward the house. "I'll start a long, long letter, the longest I have ever written."

Chapter Two

It was the right kind of a day on the morrow. In front of Mama on the writing desk was a sheet of white paper. The sky was very blue as she gazed out at it. She did not know in her mind if the place where dear Papa's soul was dwelling could be called outer space. No one but God knew. But it really did not matter. All she wanted was some tangible thing on which to fasten her thoughts. And it was lovely to think of eternity as somewhere up in the blue sky.

So, when she was writing the letter, Mama would think upward. After all, she calculated, each person had a right to form his own thought-world, true to that inner feeling that made thoughts come and go. There might be many other persons who, heartsick for loved ones, feel like writing to them. Setting down your longings and thoughts was a great release, even if it seemed unreal and a bit fantastic. She had a right to do it, and somehow, she felt, her thoughts would reach him. Believing this would give her joy and be the mainspring of her motive for writing.

There was a prayer in Mama's heart, a prayer of thankfulness for the husband who had belonged to her for so many years and for the children with whom God had blessed them. Eight of them! All were now fine well-educated men and women, doing their best to fulfill their special missions in life. Suddenly her prayer became a psalm, soft music that sometimes took a gay high note, and sometimes melted into tranquillity. That musical prayer would be the wordless perface to her letter. And so, Mama picked up her pen and began:

Dear Papa:

It was so long ago that we climbed Gellivara together. But I remember well those last happy hours as we joked and laughed, sitting there on that mountain slope in Lapland. Then you told me how much you loved me. I felt almost like a young girl again, a little embarrassed listening to your words because I was not used to hearing you speak them, although through the years my heart had heard them over and over. And because I knew you so well and loved you so deeply, the words that had been unsaid were already written in my heart. Still it came as a surprise to hear you really saying them. And God was good to let you utter them, because I did not know then that you were going to leave me. And when you did, so suddenly, when your dear, wonderful heart almost stopped beating and they carried you down the mountain, I seemed to be dying with you.

Now, thinking back, I realize it was the right time. You had reached the finish line of your race of life. There were no long hours of suffering or struggling. You just let go . . . and there you were with God in His eternity.

I have a feeling now that my own race is almost finished, that soon I shall be with you and that will be so wonderful. I am so excited about it and so curious. What is it like where you are, I wonder, and what is that life that never ends? Suddenly it seems that I can't wait for that moment to come. You know, darling, how impatient I always was about waiting for something. I feel I'd like to pray, "Please, God, don't let me wait too long."

I have finished my work. Our "dreams" have grown up. Seven of them have their own families, and the one who never married has a host of friends and the joy of being in a place where she can give to those who thirst for knowledge.

I have so much, so very much to tell you. I have this dear little home where I have lived alone with my memories, and where so many dear friends drop in and so many people who have needed me come in for prayer and comfort. I know that I have carried on your work in my own way, giving and doing and helping, and that the minister's wife I wanted to become when I was young was really my calling. I was true to it, Pontus, and I hope that you are pleased.

It was so right for me to live here. My health has been good despite that heart attack. My eyes are beginning to wear out though. I don't like to admit it, but it is a little hard for me to see. The doctor told me that no glasses can help any more. It would be hard for me not to be able to see to write. Writing letters and receiving them has always been a joy. So, I'd like to leave this world while I can still move and do my own work and live in my own house. God knows that, and I am sure he will answer my prayer to die well. I don't think it is selfish not to want to suffer. I think it is the way it should be, to die with life still full to the brim and overflowing.

This letter will be about our children, not just what has taken place since you left, but many things I had saved for us to share in our old age. Things happened that you never knew because, darling, you were so strict with the children, I was afraid they would be punished. But I can tell you now.

Of all the children, Torkel is the one who looks most like his Papa. Now, when his hair is beginning to recede, he is more like you than ever. It isn't just his looks; it's his ways. He has that same quiet, almost shy, way about him; he never wants to push forward into the limelight. He seems happiest just serving the members of his church. Promotions and honors seem to hold no interest for him. He works for his church and his family. Nancy and Torkel have two fine sons, you see. He is a fine preacher, and so easy to listen to. Sometimes I can close my eyes and imagine that it is your voice speaking.

Our Torkel was a good little boy, but unknown to his Papa he very often meddled in things he had no business to bother with, such as his Papa's ministry. But I sometimes thought that he succeeded where you failed. Your pride would have been wounded had I told you at the time. That, my dearest, is why I hid these things deep in my heart, thinking that when Torkel has grown to be a man I could tell you about them and we could laugh together and perhaps thank God, too. But when that time came, darling, you were not here to tell. But this I want you to know; whatever Torkel did, he did to help you because you were his hero, his ideal. He was striving to become like you when he grew up.

One of these incidents happened when he was ten years old, an eager, blond little boy who let his thoughts go deeper than we ever realized. No, you could not have taken the truth just then. But a Mama is made differently from a Papa. She can see beyond the years and in her heart she knows that things which at the time seem like the wrong turn in the road for a little boy, can be the making of him if handled in a wise way.

It had been a busy summer in Berkley Hills that year. The Franzons had just returned from their vacation in New Sweden, Maine. At this beautiful, picturesque spot both Mama and Papa had had a spell of

28

homesickness for Sweden because the place reminded them so much of the old country. There were still a couple of weeks left of the school vacation as they took up life in the city again.

Calle and Torkel were extremely busy those weeks because they had entered a contest offered by the Nature Museum in the large city park to see which boy could bring the most interesting specimen. It must be something he had found or caught himself. So, the cellar had begun to fill up with boxes housing toads, worms, mice, birds, and all kinds of crawling things. These had to be nursed and fed so they would be strong and flawless on that big day when the boys would choose some of them to enter the contest. When Torkel found a wounded snake their excitement soared high. But how could anyone in the Franzon household have known that this snake that some driver had carelessly run over, would one day become a mission snake and do special evangelistic work for a preacher? And it was all old Mrs. Malmstrom's fault from the beginning.

There was sadness over the little church. Mrs. Malmstrom, who some years before had been saved from alcohol, had suddenly begun to drink heavily again. Time after time she had been found on unsteady legs. Papa had talked and prayed with her over and over again, but to no avail. At the last deacon's meeting it had been decided to strike her name from the list of church members. But first she was to have three chances to repent: one, a week of prayers offered just for her by the faithful church members; another, a call from the board of deacons; and the third, Papa preaching a powerful sermon just for her benefit.

The week of prayer had come and gone without seeming to make any impression on the fallen woman. The deacons had fulfilled their mission, talking in serious, concerned words about the discipline of the church. They had made it clear that, if she had not repented by the time of the next business meeting, her name would be taken from the list of the faithful mem-

29

bers of Papa's church. She had cried then and promised, but the very next day reports had reached the head deacon that she was drunk again.

"There is only my sermon left now," sighed Papa as he stood by the kitchen table which Mama was setting for supper.

"Poor, poor Mrs. Malmstrom," said Mama, wiping a tear from her eye. "I can't see that throwing her out of the church is going to help her in any way."

"No, it isn't to help, Maria." Papa's voice was firm. "But the church has a standard to live up to, a holy, glorious task. It must be an example to the world, or it has lost its calling. You know that things like this always hurt me deep in my soul, but we have tried every method we know and if there was one ounce of will power in her, she would try."

"How do we know how much she tries or how hard the temptations are that she is fighting within herself, Pontus?" pleaded Mama. "I think the church should help and stand by her instead of washing its hands of her and letting the poor woman go to destruction."

Papa walked out of the kitchen with slow, even steps. Mama knew his heart was heavy. It was not always easy to be a pastor in a church like the one Papa served, one that had made a pledge before the Lord to live up to its calling.

Presently the cellar door was pushed open and Torkel came into the kitchen.

"I heard, Mama," he said, looking up at her with bewilderment written on his face. "I heard Papa say that they were going to throw Mrs. Malmstrom out of the church because she gets drunk."

Mama felt a wave of compassion going out to her son. No wonder he was confused. In better times they had often been invited to dinner in Mrs. Malmstrom's nice home. Torkel could remember the whole family sitting around her dining-room table in the days before Mr. Malmstrom had died. The dinners had been happy occasions. Later on the boys had done little errands for her and they had always been rewarded. How could a boy ten years old understand the church's discipline and its way of dealing with sin?

Torkel looked thoughtful. "Is Papa preaching the powerful sermon next Sunday, Mama?" he asked.

"Yes, Torkel, it has to be done as soon as that."

"Could I help him, do you think?"

Mama smiled. "No, darling. This is Papa's work and he will have to do it alone like the preacher he is. His topic will be 'Man's First Temptation.' I know you know the story told in the book of Genesis about how that serpent tempted God's first people to fall."

Torkel nodded. All the parsonage children read a chapter of the Bible each day.

"What do you think would happen, Mama," Torkel ventured, "if suddenly, when Papa was preaching, a snake, a real live snake, came before Mrs. Malmstrom's eyes? Do you think that would make her repent?"

"Perhaps it would, darling. But don't be so concerned. You're much too young to worry about things you don't understand. Just let us pray that Papa's sermon will be so powerful that Mrs. Malmstrom can really see that terrible serpent within her heart and that she will get the power to overcome her sin."

After Torkel had gone down cellar again, Mama could not help thinking what an unusual boy he was for his years. He was really so concerned about this poor woman that he wanted to help if he could find a way. Surely Torkel would grow up to be a preacher like his Papa; Mama was convinced of that.

Torkel did not say any more about Mrs. Malmstrom, but Mama thought that at times he looked very thoughtful and she had a feeling the problem was very much on his young mind. She said nothing to Papa about it, however. She felt that he had enough to worry about and she knew he was working hard to shape up that powerful sermon that he hoped would turn a fallen woman into a saint.

On that very important Sunday morning there was a

slight gloom over the parsonage. Papa talked very little and Mama did her best to keep her children quiet and well behaved. Torkel's eyes followed her wherever she went. Just before leaving for church he approached her with a heavy brown paper bag in his hand. "This is my project I am taking with me to church today, Mama," he informed her.

Very often the children took work to do in Sunday school after church, so Mama did not see anything unusual about it. She just smiled at his eager face. That boy certainly put his whole heart into anything he undertook.

Papa had made sure that Mrs. Malmstrom would be in church this morning. He had phoned to tell her that they would call for her. She was invited to sit with the family and come home for dinner at the parsonage after the service. No effort would be spared to make this a successful meeting.

Mrs. Malmstrom was waiting, dressed in her best.

"Can I sit beside you in church, Mrs. Malmstrom?" Torkel asked as they began their ride toward the church.

Mrs. Malmstrom looked very pleased. "Of course you can, Torkel. You might have to poke me at times. I fall asleep so easily these days when I sit in a warm cozy place and I hear a voice talking for a long time."

She is trying in her own way to ask us to make sure she hears every word Papa preaches, Mama thought happily. Oh, this would work! She felt sure of it.

The eyes of the congregation were on them as they filed into the second pew where the pastor's family always sat. Mama hoped that kindly thoughts would surround them every minute of this sacred hour.

The service got off to a good start. The church was almost filled. Papa looked stately and dignified and he often glanced over at their pew. Once Mama looked in the direction of their guest. She was nodding already. But Torkel, although he seemed to be aware of this, made no effort to poke her. Then it happened and if

32

Mama's eyes had not been on them at that moment, she would have never known. Torkel opened Mrs. Malmstrom's pocketbook and slipped inside it something from his paper bag. Luckily Mrs. Malmstrom always carried a large purse. But what had Torkel given her so silently and mysteriously?

Mama's eyes turned back to Papa as eloquent words flowed from his lips, words full of life and power. Never had she heard him make a story of sin so real. But Torkel was still neglecting to awaken Mrs. Malmstrom. Mama looked at him penetratingly and suddenly his eyes met hers. She motioned him to give Mrs. Malmstrom that poke she had asked for. He got her sign and she saw him move closer and closer to Mrs. Malmstrom, who straightened up and smiled at him. She listened now to Papa's words, falling just like blows from a hammer.

"Temptation is the thing that mars our world today," he said, "and because we are weak and without backbone or courage, we fall and the devil has his way in many hearts. I would to God that He would allow us to open our spiritual eyes and see the evil around us in the form of a serpent, tempting us to wander from God's way. Perhaps then . . ."

Mama saw a tear roll down Mrs. Malmstrom's cheek, as she grabbed her pocketbook and opened it, evidently to take out her handkerchief. This sermon was really finding its target. Suddenly Mama saw something that made her blood chill. A snake's beady eyes looked out of Mrs. Malmstrom's pocketbook and then, quick as a wink, it slithered from the large handbag to freedom, wiggling its way down under the church pews to . . . well, Mama never knew where, because Mrs. Malmstrom had covered her face and cried out loud like a child as her tears flowed without stopping.

Papa cut his sermon short. The work was accomplished and when the deacons met with the sinner, after the service, she promised that never would a drop of liquor touch her lips again.

Dinner that day was the happiest one Mama could ever remember in the parsonage with a guest present. But Torkel's face shone the brightest.

Later on, when Calle complained that the prize snake for the museum exhibition had mysteriously disappeared from its box in the cellar Mama acted as if she knew nothing. But Torkel, although he was mute before Calle, explained the lost snake to Mama.

"Don't tell Papa," he pleaded. "Let him think his powerful sermon did it. It was a strong sermon, Mama, that made you afraid to sin. We lost the specimen that I'm sure could have given us the museum prize, but I offered it for the mission, Mama. Perhaps this snake had to make up for that other one that made those first people bad. My snake made Mrs. Malmstrom good."

And that woman never again touched a drop of destroying drink. She was true to her promise. And it was all, thought Mama, because another promise had come true: "And a little child shall lead them."

It took Mama a long, long time to get snakes out of her mind and whenever Mrs. Malmstrom sat in front of her in church and opened her large pocketbook, Mama got chills up and down her spine. And there were mornings at the parsonage when Papa in his deep, sincere voice lifted up Mrs. Malmstrom's victory in a prayer of thanks, and Mama had a guilty feeling in her heart because she had not told Papa how Mrs. Malmstrom had been converted from drinking. But loyalty to Torkel kept her silent. There had been something so very special in the generous way he had offered that snake on the altar for a mission that she did not want him to be punished for it. And Papa surely would not have spared the rod if the story had reached his ears. It would have wounded his preaching pride deeply. Mama found it was not easy to be torn between a husband and a son and she hoped that soon time would throw its gentle mantle over the snake episode and perhaps as the years rolled by, it would fade from her memory.

But a few weeks later, when Torkel informed her

that he was starting a new project to help Papa, she was on her guard. And when she realized that he had become convinced that he was a "do-gooder" and threatened to be filled with righteous indignation whenever he found the opportunity, she knew she had to put a stop to it.

This new project involved Dr. Smith, for whom Torkel worked, and some wine bottles he kept in his basement.

"I am working on a plan to empty them, Mama," Torkel confided in her, "and fill them with clean colored water that will not hurt anyone."

Mama had had a long talk with him that night and it was a good talk. And even if he seemed a bit confused about the concern Mama showed at this special mission, he promised to talk it over with Papa first. Mama felt much better after that because she wanted to be sure she was leading her little ones on the right road. But she was not surprised that Torkel looked bewildered. At times she herself was puzzled as to what was right or wrong for a Mama to do when the Papa was left out.

Chapter Three

Each day, as Mama tore a new page from the calendar on her desk, it seemed to her that April got warmer and warmer. It was at this time of the year in Miami that Mama missed springtime, not so much New England springs as those she remembered in Sweden.

35

Spring in Sweden was something wonderful. The twilight became longer and longer each day and the mystery of new life slowly became evident in all nature. It was that stirring of things beginning to bud and come to life, and of water rushing down the mountain slopes, and of air warmed by the spring sun that transformed a frozen world into a fairyland where the longing heart found its place. Sweden must still be like that, thought Mama. But now she was a part of America. She had chosen to live in Florida, and Florida made up for so much with its balmy winters that she hardly remembered the cold, stormy falls and the long snowy winters of her Lapland.

She had finished her housework and sat down again to talk to Papa.

Dear, dear Pontus:

A glow from the yesteryears is still shining on me as I begin to write on my letter to you. It seems that when I think of those wonderful years we had together, memories step out of the shadows of time and become so real that I am living them over again.

Yes, time seems like the hand of a clock that slowly moves back, bringing bright pictures into view. Do you remember, darling, how concerned we were about Vickey, fresh out of high school, falling head over heels in love with John, the new preacher who had just graduated from the Seminary? And all the while, you and I had been so sure it was going to be John and Button. Perhaps that was a wish dear to my heart because I always worried about Button. One never knew what she would do next and having her anchored down to a preacher would have taken away much of the strain and worry about her future. It was foolish of me, for Button had made it clear that she never wanted to follow in my steps and become a minister's wife.

Well, Vickey certainly solved that problem for her. We had wanted Vickey to go to college and it wasn't easy to let her go ahead with that beautiful wedding. But we never regretted it. And, Pontus, I am happy to tell you that John has moved from one church to another, each one a little bigger than the last. That small church in Littlemont was just a starting point. Now he has a large church in Minnesota and Vickey—well let me tell you, although she has had a home and three children to care for, and her duties as a minister's wife, she has finished college and even holds a Master's degree. Where there's a will there's a way and Vickey, who was so quiet and gentle, has a stronger will than we ever realized.

But I would like to tell you a story about Vickey from way back in the farm years. It seems like a dream that there was a time when you, Pontus, could no longer take the ministry, when coming to a new country had been too much for you, and when you took a two-year leave of absence and bought that little farm in New England. And what a darling farm it was, just big enough, with the farmhouse on the top of the hill and the lovely lake below and the brook bubbling down at one side of the house. It belongs among my loveliest memories.

All the children were young then, although the three oldest were old enough to be a great help to us. But wasn't the farm a wonderful idea and with so much space for the children to run around and play without any limitations! It wasn't at all hard to be transformed from a minister's wife to a farmer's mate. How well we worked together with the chores—even the milking, after I got over being frightened of those fierce-looking cows.

I'm glad we never gave up the dignity of the parsonage, that it followed us to the country. I wanted to do things there the same way I had always done them. You know that entertaining was my pet pleasure. But there was one day when that dignified entertaining could have had grave consequences if God's angels had not been there to protect our Greta.

The spring sunshine was pouring into the large farm kitchen where Mama was baking fancy pastries. It seemed to Vickey, who was playing in one corner with her sister, Greta, that Mama had been flying about with lightning speed, doing a hundred things at once, since early morning when there had been a telephone call from some of the prominent ladies of the Berkley Hills church where Papa had been serving. They wanted to come to the farm for a visit. And Mama had, of course, invited them for afternoon coffee.

Company was Mama's delight and she always cleaned and baked and fussed when guests were expected. She had made up her mind that entertaining on the farm must have the same grace and dignity it had always had in the parsonage. She must show the ladies that being a farmer's wife had not changed her one bit. And this first visit would be the most important one. Today all the children were busy in their own way. The three youngest were playing in the big sand pile Papa had put in the corner of the garden so Mama could keep an eye on them from the kitchen window. Greta and Vickey were in the kitchen, and Pelle, Nim, and Button were helping Papa with the farm chores.

Vickey had been watching Mama for a long time. Mama's cheeks were rosy and her blue eyes were shining like stars. Her hands, thought Vickey, seemed to love to do nice things.

"Mama," she said softly, "are you going to use the hand-painted coffee cups today, the ones we brought from Sweden?"

"Of course I am," laughed Mama gaily, "and the old silver service, too. This is a very special party, darling."

"Will there be any little girls coming, Mama?"

"Not this time, Vickey. You and Greta must help me a little now, then after lunch you can go outdoors and play all afternoon."

"We'll put our dolls away now, Mama. What do you want us to do?"

"I want you to dust in the dining room, girls, and do the chairs especially well. You know those ladies have very good eyes."

The girls did the dusting and Mama placed a crisp white tablecloth on the round dining-room table, and began to place the wafer-thin cups on a tray.

Vickey was thinking that it seemed just like playing when Mama worked at something. She wished that she would be grown up soon, so she could have a home and do all the things that Mama did. It looked like so much fun.

There was a quick luncheon for the family and then Mama sent the girls out to play without having them help her with the dishes.

"You're spoiling them, Maria," Papa said.

"I don't have time to have them poking around the kitchen today, Pontus *lilla*," Mama answered sweetly. "I can do it so much faster myself."

Papa laughed. "Maria," he said suddenly, "I was just thinking. It's good to be a farmer and not be compelled to go to ladies' parties. But I can still have some of those fancy *vienerbröd*."

"Now, Pontus, you look like a little boy who skipped school to go fishing. I want to remind you that there might come a time when you will long for those coffee parties. Anyway, you'd better not stray too far from your old life; there's always a coming back, you know."

Mama blew Papa a kiss as he walked out the door to go back to his chores. She could not help thinking how well he looked today. The farm was doing him a lot of good.

Vickey and Greta played near the house for a while. They saw the ladies arrive and watched Mama greet them with open arms at the front door. She had changed into a blue dress that matched her eyes. There was a lot of talking and sometimes Mama's happy laughter rolled like a silvery melody out into the yard where the girls played.

"Let's play down by the brook, Vickey," suggested Greta. "We can make believe we're fishing."

"We could borrow Papa's bamboo poles, but I don't think we'd better," answered Vickey. "Let's find our own sticks."

Soon the girls had their sticks and some string, and they hurried down to the brook. It was an enchanting spot to play, there on that rickety old wooden bridge where the brook was so noisy as it gurgled down, jumping over stones until it reached the lake.

The boards groaned and creaked as the girls leaned over the railing holding their homemade fishing tackle. It was lots of fun!

Suddenly Vickey's eyes began to sparkle.

"Do you see what I see, Greta?" she whispered hoarsely. "It's a crawfish . . . a real live crawfish. I wish Papa was here so he could catch it for us."

Greta leaned forward and stared, too. "I can't see it, Vickey. Where?"

"It's right by that big stone. It's crawling backwards. See?"

But Greta could not see it. She leaned over even farther and suddenly there was a crackling sound, and the railing and Greta both tumbled into the bubbling brook.

"Help! Help!" Greta screamed. "I'm drowning! Save me, Vickey!"

"I can't reach you, Greta. If I lean any farther, I'll fall in, too. I'll run fast to get Mama. Just hold your head up! Don't let it get under the water! And, Greta, pray . . . pray hard until Mama comes."

Vickey raced up the hill, across the lawn, up onto the porch, in through the front door, and right into the living room where Mama was gracefully pouring coffee into the beautiful Swedish coffee cups. She ran straight to the table, pushing past the ladies to reach Mama.

40

"Mama, Mama," she cried. "Mama, Greta——"

Mama looked at Vickey and there was fire in her eyes. She did not say a word, but touched her finger to her lips and Vickey knew that she must not talk until Mama gave her permission to. She walked slowly back to the door and sat down on a chair, but her eyes clung to Mama's face. Please, please, they pleaded, speak to me, Mama, or we might not have a Greta.

But Mama poured the coffee for all the ladies and not until they had all been served, did she excuse herself and walk over to Vickey.

Vickey felt as though she had been sitting on needles. Her body was all sore and shaky. But to her surprise, Mama grabbed her by the arm and ushered her out of the room into a corner of the hall where she spoke in an angry voice.

"How could you do it, Vickey? You spoiled my nice party. You were very rude, pushing your way to the table and screaming at the top of your voice. And after all the instructions I gave you about playing nicely. Now you can not even have one cooky."

"I don't want any cookies, Mama," sobbed Vickey. "I think Greta is all swallowed up now, but please come anyway, Mama. Greta fell into the brook from the rickety bridge . . ."

Mama's eyes filled with fear as she stared at her daughter. And the next moment she darted out through the door.

"Tell the ladies that I will be back, Vickey. Tell them anything, then come and help me. Oh, poor dear Greta . . . Oh!" Mama moaned.

Vickey hurriedly obeyed Mama's order. Rushing back into the living room, she pulled herself up to her full height. She wanted to do this right. It was terrible for Mama to have to leave and fish Greta from the brook on this very special afternoon. They should never have gone down to the brook. But it was too late now.

"Please, ladies," she cried out, "Mama had to go on

41

an important errand, but she will be right back. It is a family problem. But she wants you to help yourselves over and over again and eat for a long time. And now I have to run, too."

She ran very fast, trying to catch up with Mama who had already reached the bridge. Mama was staring horrified at the broken railing, looking in vain into the water for Greta.

Vickey stood beside her with tears running down her cheeks. "Oh, Mama, she's gone. She must have drowned all the way down in the lake."

Mama and Vickey were almost at the end of the brook when a strange sound reached their ears. Someone was singing. The sound came up from the side of the brook: "The Lord leads the way through the wilderness, all I have to do is follow . . ." and before they had time to take another step:

"Jesus, Savior, pilot me. Over life's tempestuous sea."

They both stared. Greta was clinging to a slim branch of a tree that hung down over the water. The stream was carrying her down to the lake and she looked like a drowned rat with her dripping wet hair and her face red from the icy water.

It took Mama a few moments to get her out of the water.

"Darling, darling," she cried, hugging the child to her. "Oh, I'm so glad we found you safe."

Mama's pretty blue dress was all wet now, but she was happy to see Greta smiling through her tears.

"It wasn't very deep, Mama, but there were those big stones and every time I tried to climb out, I slipped and the water kept washing me downstream. I thought you never would come."

Mama sighed. "It was my fault, honey, but now you're safe . . . and to think that you could keep singing. Oh, Greta, you are wonderful!"

"Vickey told me to pray," Greta said, "and I prayed

so long that I ran out of words, but it didn't seem to help. Then, as soon as I started singing, you came."

Mama and Vickey and Greta started the long wet walk back to the farmhouse. Mama was glad Papa was nowhere in sight. How could she ever explain Greta's adventure in the brook on this, the afternoon of the fancy coffee party?

When they came up to the farmhouse Mama found the ladies standing on the front veranda looking in all directions, very much alarmed.

"They know something awful has happened," said Mama. "Now, girls, let me do the talking."

"What in the world, Maria?" The ladies sounded as though they had practiced a chorus.

Mama laughed happily, though God knew how sad and upset she still felt inside.

"Our Greta decided to jump in the brook and let the Lord pilot her down to the sea. But Vickey wanted me there to see that she made it safely. And she did. But now, ladies, excuse me while I stick her in the tub for a hot bath and into bed. You never know what one youngster will think up to do when you have eight of them . . . and at the wrong time, too. I hope Pastor Franzon never hears of this. He hasn't the patience with them that I have. Go back into the parlor please, ladies. I will have a cup of coffee with you all in a few minutes."

Mama had talked so fast that the ladies did not have time to ask questions. And she knew she was safe when they trotted back into the living room. Mama put the coffeepot on the stove and then put Greta into the tub.

Later on when Greta was in bed under a pile of blankets and the ladies had departed, Mama rehearsed what she would tell Papa. She couldn't help smiling to herself when she thought of Greta. That singing, coming from the brook, had been one of the strangest things she had ever heard.

But surely Greta had been piloted through the

waters, and led through the wilderness. And Mama knew, as always, that her children knew where to turn in time of trouble.

Chapter Four

Here in her little white bungalow, with most of her life behind her, Mama lived in a magic world, a world divided between dreams and reality. In her garden the many trees and plants and flowers seemed to be trying to outdo each other in loveliness. And today, after one of those extremely hot spells, a cool rain had drenched the earth and the wind blew the tops of the palm trees, which made a longing, restless sound that found an echo in Mama's own heart. It was as though she couldn't wait until June when she would leave on her trip East to see four of her children and their families.

Emma Ostrom, a good friend who had also come from the old country, was always within reach by telephone if Mama needed help with her housework. It used to be once a week during the hot season, but lately Mama had been calling her twice and sometimes even three times a week.

"There's so much to be done, Emma," Mama confided to her friend one night when the day's work was finished and Emma was leaving for home. "If you can, come back tomorrow. I want every bit of the house gone over before I leave on my trip. Everything must be in perfect order. There are lots of things we must throw out or give away . . . You see, I have a strange feeling that I might not return and I want my children to find my house in the kind of order about which I always preached to them when they were growing up."

Emma looked at Mama for a moment before she spoke. Then she said, "Maria, I should tell you not to talk like that, but you alone know what you feel in your heart. I'll gladly give you all the time you want and together we'll have your home shining from top to bottom. But I hope you're wrong about not coming back. You belong in this little house, near all of us who love you so dearly. But if your Maker calls you, I know you're ready to leave."

Mama smiled happily, glad that her friend understood.

"I'm writing a long letter, Emma, and when I get it ready I want you to keep it for me. It's not to be opened unless my premonition comes true. If I don't return, please mail it to Button. She will understand why I wrote it.

Emma promised to do what Mama asked of her. The letter would be a sacred document entrusted to her and Mama knew it would be safe in her keeping.

That night turned out to be one of those unbearably hot ones, and Mama, awakening in the wee hours, was unable to go back to sleep. There was a strange restlessness within her as thoughts and memories rushed through her mind. She turned on her bed lamp and picked up her Bible. Reading a chapter from this sacred book had always made her still and at peace before, but tonight it seemed to make her even more awake.

Finally Mama stepped out of bed, threw a light negligee over her nightgown, and walked out into the living room. Soon the whole house was lit up and the sheets of white paper on the desk seemed to be calling to her.

I must write some more on my letter to Pontus, she thought. I seem to be living more in the past than in the present. There's so much to write him and it seems as if time is running out. After all, I can sleep late in the morning, so if I feel like writing tonight, why shouldn't I?

Presently the doorbell chimed. For a moment Mama was frightened. Who would be calling on her at this time of the night? But then she knew. It must be Nim! He must have seen her house all lit up and stopped to see if something was wrong. She glanced out at the street and, sure enough, there stood his Cadillac with its lights shinging brightly, indicating that he would only stay for a minute.

Mama opened the door. "Nim," she laughed, "what a time to call on your mother!"

"And what is my Mama doing up at this hour? I was on my way home from the hospital—an accident case —and I felt anxious when I saw your house all lit up like a Christmas tree."

Mama gave Nim a light kiss on the cheek. "Relax, son, all is well. I couldn't sleep, so I just decided to get out of bed and think a little. That's all."

"Good," said Nim, still standing in the doorway. "I'll run home and catch a little sleep before another day's work begins. I'm glad you're all right. But what a funny Mama to get up in the middle of the night just to do some thinking."

Mama waved him off. It was good of Nim to stop. She was always grateful for her children's concern over her.

As she sat down at the desk, Mama's mind was clear and alert. She didn't want to wait another minute to continue writing to Pontus. It was as though she was living only to finish this long letter before she began to pack to go away for the summer.

Papa darling:

Here I am again and this time it is in the deep of the night that I am writing to you. I feel almost as though there is not enough time. I alarmed Nim with a lighted house as he was coming from the hospital a few moments ago, so I had a short visit

46

with him. I didn't tell him that my reason for leaving my bed was this burning desire to talk to you.

Pontus, you, too, would be proud to see how well Nim has done as a doctor. People love him. He always seems to have time to let them open their hearts to him, and sometimes that is where the root of the sickness lies. A doctor is sometimes even closer to a person than their minister. Perhaps you would not like to have me say that, but I know it's true. Sometimes a heart has to bear too much and there is no pain as sharp and severe as a heart pain. But when a person can open up and tell all, sometimes that helps more than medicine. I know that Nim carries so much of people's lives, not just in his skillful hands when he operates, but in his heart as he feels compassion for them. A doctor like that really serves God in the capacity of a minister. He also has been called to do God's bidding here on earth.

Nim's practice is getting bigger and bigger and Karin has been a wonderful help to him. She is still beautiful and the years have only added a certain sweetness to her lovely face. Their three children are grown now and I have great grand-children to love, three of them with red hair. Isn't that wonderful, darling? Yes, Nim truly followed his calling and his heart's sincere desire, although you always wanted him to be a preacher and fol-low in your steps. I think he has combined the two and it has made him a great man, more than his Papa could have asked for.

Growing up seemed a very natural thing to Nim, Pontus. He was your right hand and how proud you were of that boy, never once doubting that he would follow in your footsteps. He was gifted in so many ways and speaking and express-ing himself came very easily to him. He always confided in you, but there was one time that I re-

47

member very plainly, Pontus, when he opened up his young heart to me. Nim was afraid that he had failed you in a very important task. This little episode I never told you about, for I don't know how you would have taken it. It was a small incident, but to us in the parsonage even small incidents sometimes became very important.

The Franzons had been in America only one year, but it had been a tremendous one in many ways. It had taken Papa quite a while to get used to the small Swedish church there and although Mama was always bubbling over with excitement about opportunities in this golden land, and the children seemed to enter in with all their vim and vigor, Papa did not feel that he had accomplished as much as he had planned to in his work as a preacher. A pastor did not have the authority here that he did in Sweden. Big things were decided by the church boards and committees and sometimes he felt that aside from preaching and counseling duties, a pastor here could easily become a mere figurehead. Well, he would not let that happen to him. If it did, he would resign and go back to his beloved Sweden, no matter how much Mama objected.

Then one day an important letter arrived. A great honor was about to be bestowed on the little church. Pastor Olof Oskarsson, President of the Swedish Conference, was coming for a visit. He was anxious to see how the new minister from Sweden was coming along. He mentioned a night when he would like to give a talk in the church and stay at the parsonage. For the first time since Papa came to Berkley Hills, he began to perk up and be happy.

"We must have everything in perfect shape both in the church and the parsonage when Oskarsson arrives, Maria. We can give him our bedroom and we will sleep in the den."

"Of course we'll give him our room, Pontus, and as far as the parsonage is concerned, you need have no

48

worries about pleasing the great pastor. I'll cook a special dinner because this I know about preachers, Pontus *lilla,* whether from small or big churches or even the head of the Conference, they do love to eat."

"That I know you can handle, Maria. And I want all the children to be on the alert. I think I will give them each some little task for those two days. Pelle can carry Pastor Oskarsson's suitcase to and from his room. Torkel and Calle can see that his shoes are shined. Vickey and Greta can see that there is always water on the night table by his bed. Button can ask if there is something he wants to have pressed. And little Kerstin can just put her arms around his neck when she goes to bed and make him feel that he is one of the family."

"And Nim?" said Mama. "Pontus, you forgot Nim."

"No, I didn't, Maria. I have a very special task for Nim. I've been thinking for a long time that I would like to have my oldest son with me up on the platform sometime to begin to give him a little training in what I hope will be his future work. But I also want to show him off to our distinguished guest. I thought, Maria, that I would have Nim lead the welcome song so I would be free to escort Oskarsson up the church aisle. I'd like to walk beside him and then introduce him to the people."

"That's a wonderful plan, Pontus, and Nim will be proud to help. After all, he is almost sixteen now and such a fine boy."

Nim was thrilled at Papa's suggestion.

"You choose a hymn from the hymnbook, Nim," directed Papa, "something fitting for this glad occasion. And when you see Pastor Oskarsson and me come into the foyer—you can see us through the windows on those inside doors—then have the congregation stand up and sing with all their might. When we reach the platform, we will sit on special chairs there, and you continue with the song and then say a few words before turning the meeting over to me."

49

It was all set and both Papa and Mama felt that they had made the best possible plans for the great occasion.

The day Pastor Oskarsson was to arrive the parsonage had an air of festivity and delicious odors drifted out from the kitchen. Mama had baked and cooked and cleaned. She surely was not going to let Papa down with her part of the entertaining. Nim came out into the kitchen as she was frosting a chocolate cake for the reception in the church parlor after the service. This was one of Mama's prize recipes and it was always one of the preferred cakes among the ladies who scrambled to the table to get a taste of Maria's baking wonders.

Nim watched as Mama spread the creamy white frosting over the dark mahogany-colored cake. It looked like tiny ripples on a lake, he thought. Mama surely knew the art of baking.

"Mama," said Nim thoughtfully, holding a hymnbook in his hand, "I've been searching for a hymn for tonight by looking in the back of the book at the first lines of all the hymns. What do you think of this one, 'Come, here is Jubilee'?"

"That sounds very festive, Nim. There couldn't be a better beginning."

Mama put the cake in the pantry and placed her hand on Nim's shoulder. He was tall for his age and his red hair almost sparkled in the sunshine that came pouring in through the kitchen window. What a handsome boy he had become!

"You must not let Papa down tonight, Nim," she smiled. "Look very poised and dignified up there in the pulpit and by all means, wave your arms if you have to, so the singing will be good."

"Don't worry, Mama. I'll do my very best. I'm not a bit nervous. I will leave the number of the hymn on the organ for Mrs. Jepson. I hope she comes on time tonight. You know how it annoys Papa if she's even a half a minute late."

Mama had coffee ready when the visiting pastor arrived. He was a big man, at least six feet tall. A bright

50

fire crackled in the fireplace in the living room where Mama served the coffee. Pelle had been right on hand to carry the bags and Button had been given a pair of black pants that needed the creases pressed out. Torkel's eyes and Calle's were glued on the guest's shoes, wondering when they could get them off his feet to give them an extra good shine. Kerstin had nestled up to him lovingly and he patted her with his big, soft hand. Everything seemed to proceed in perfect order so Papa could not have any complaints later. His family were certainly doing their part to make Pastor Oskarsson's visit a delightful memory.

Mama had roast turkey with all the fixings for supper and a happy group gathered around the diningroom table.

"You certainly have a fine family, Franzon," said Pastor Oskarsson contentedly when the meal was over.

"The best there is," laughed Papa.

"The dinner was superb, but I don't know how my speech will fare after all that fine food."

"Let us go for a walk," suggested Papa. "That always seems to me to be the remedy for a full stomach."

Mama was glad for a chance to get at the dishes. She wanted time to take a last look in the church parlor to see that the candles were on the table and the teaspoons placed in the right way.

She was pleased to see the people coming early to fill the sanctuary and, as the meeting began, all the seats were filled. Nim was sitting in Papa's big chair on the platform, and Mama knew he was watching the outside door attentively. Suddenly he rose to his feet and announced the number of the hymn, asking the congregation to stand and sing with all their hearts on this glad occasion.

Mrs. Jepson, who had arrived at the last moment, struck a chord on the organ as the ushers opened the door to the foyer and Papa and Pastor Oskarsson stepped inside to begin their walk up the short church aisle. The singing boomed out in a mighty chorus:

51

"Come, here is Jubilee,"

It was a surprised Nim who, when he heard the next line, instantly realized he had been so confident that this was a song of jubilee that he had never read the rest of the words. The voices of the congregation hit his heart like a bombshell as they sang out:

> *"Sinner, come home,*
> *Sinner, come home."*

Mama's heart almost stopped beating. Why hadn't she read through the song? How could she have been so foolish as to let Nim have a free hand? Oh, what would Papa do now? He must feel terrible. She did not even dare to look his way.

The pastors had reached the platform and seated themselves in the big chairs. Nim's face became as red as his hair as the song boomed louder and louder and it seemed that it would never end. There were four long verses and following every other line came the awful words:

> *"Sinner, come home.*
> *Sinner, come home."*

Mama could see Papa's eyes shooting flames and it seemed to her that Pastor Oskarsson was having a hard time keeping a straight face. Finally it was over. The organ stopped and the silence that hung over the church seemed unbearable. Mama's heart cried out as poor Nim began to speak. What in the world could he say to right such a wrong?

"Distinguished guest, Papa, church members, and friends," Nim began, and Mama could see his face getting redder and redder, but there was not a quiver in his voice. It rang calm and clear: "We have just sung a great hymn about the mission of our church to bring

52

into its fellowship all sinners whether they are church members or outsiders. This is our most important task. Now let us sing from our hearts the gladness we feel at having in our church tonight the beloved president of our whole conference. Let us sing our thanks to God for Pastor Oskarsson's presence: 'Praise God from whom all blessings flow . . .'"

Mama could see the expression on Papa's face change into almost a smile. And Pastor Oskarsson suddenly looked very much moved. Never had she heard the Doxology ring out in such gladsome tones. It seemed as though the rafters would be lifted right off the roof.

In his talk the guest pastor thanked Nim for his fine beginning.

"I have to admit," he said, "that as I began to march up that aisle, the Jubilee hymn sort of took me off guard. And I wondered a little about the meaning of this unusual welcome. But now I stand amazed at the foresight of such a young brother in the work, for Nim was not thinking of the praise of men, but of our great mission as a church. I'd like to thank him for that lesson."

Much later that night, when everyone else in the parsonage had gone to bed, Mama was straightening up the last details in her kitchen when she heard the door from the dining room open and there, in his pajamas, stood Nim looking a little crestfallen.

"Mama," he said, "I think you're the only one who understood what a spot I was in tonight. I'd never read all the words of that hymn. The beginning seemed so perfect, but the rest of it was a surprise to me. I almost went out of my mind when we were singing. And to see the look on Pastor Oskarsson's face when we welcomed him over and over again with the words: 'Sinner, come home; sinner, come home'! I knew I had to do something or I would have run from the platform to hide somewhere. But I couldn't let Papa down in my first job of helping him in the ministry, so I did the best I could. Did I do right, Mama?"

Mama's arms went around her son. "Darling," she whispered, "you couldn't have done a finer job. I worried, Nim, for one horrible moment because, of course, I knew right away you never would have picked a hymn like that if you had read the words. But you fooled even the two parsons. They thought you had planned it that way and you heard how pleased our guest was."

"Yes, Mama," said Nim humbly. "And the best thing is that only you and I know it."

"And God," said Mama softly. "I think He took over, Nim."

After Nim had gone to bed, Mama said her prayer of thanks. She was so grateful for her oldest son. What insight he showed even at this age! Surely someday that boy would become a great man.

Mama folded the white paper and put it in the big envelope with the other sections of her letter. Slowly she walked back into her bedroom. She was drowsy now, but there was a happy song in her heart. How long ago that had been when Nim had come to her. And as the years sped by, she had seen with her own eyes how God had surely blessed him. Perhaps if he had not called on her on this night, the incident would never have come back to her mind. But now she had shared that, too, with Pontus.

The little house was quiet when the bright morning sun shone in at the windows of the bedroom. Mama slept on and on, and when she awoke, she felt rested and refreshed as though she had had a long vacation. The restlessness had left her and she felt more relaxed than she had in months. This letter surely was having a strange effect on her; it was a wonderful tonic. But today she would not write. She would rest from thinking of the past. She would work a little in her garden and set some coffeebread. And when it was ready, and the aroma of the baking filled her house, she would call some of her friends together for a real Swedish garden coffee party.

Life was sweet, she thought, each day so full of new adventures, and growing old did not change that at all.

Chapter Five

Mama did not write any more on her letter for several weeks. Never had she been busier than she was these days. There had been parties to go to and many functions in the church she loved so much, the one where she had been a member since she moved to Miami. And she had had parties in her own home. This was one thing she felt she had to do: be sure that she returned all the invitations and invited a few people whom she knew were lonely and who were very seldom invited to parties.

"I think you're overdoing it, Maria," scolded her friend Emma, as they were baking cookies on one of the hottest days.

"Pooh," laughed Mama. "I'm feeling wonderful, better than I have in years. And it's so much fun, Emma. I want to live life to the fullest and just now I feel almost young again. Life is so full of wonderful things."

"All right, Maria, I'm not going to try to stop you. But I've a feeling that one of these days Dr. Nim will. You're supposed to rest every day, remember?"

Mama thought about Emma's words. Perhaps she

was doing too much. How could she expect Emma or Nim or anyone else to know that she was doing all these things because she was feeling exactly the way she had when the family had left Lapland to move to America years ago. In those days, too, she had hurried, hurried, hurried to do all the things she must do, for she might never see her old friends again. She was moving far, far away. She wanted to leave the old life with a clear conscience that she had fulfilled her obligations to the smallest detail.

Yes, Mama was feeling that same way, for these things seemed just as important to her now. When she left on her trip, her heart must be light and gay and she must feel free, knowing that she had completed all she had always meant to do. Only that way could her heart feel right.

But she tried to rest a little each day, and soon she began to cut down on her activities. And so, one lovely evening as she sat in her garden, she had a pad and pen with her and she began to talk to Papa on paper again. She had missed not talking to her Pontus all these days.

Dear Papa:

Today as I thought of you, I was saying to myself, "There is no death!" For, my dearest, I have been as close to you during these times when I have written to you as I ever was before.

It is true that I cannot feel your hand hold mine or feel your face close to me and your dear voice does not speak to me as before. But the heart, Pontus, is closer than the mind or the voice or the touch, and the heart holds all those memories that only you and I can share. Together we can walk down memory's lane, side by side, hand in hand. There is no one else in the whole wide world who can remember but us.

My heart thrills when I remember Button. Pontus, she was our heartache. I shed so many tears because of her. She was a troublemaker and always so unpredictable. But now she has become an author, writing one book after another. And she claims it's just a hobby, for her home is her castle, and her family, her joy and happiness. She has her Mama's way of keeping house and is the same kind of cook. But how could we have known that when she swept things under the kitchen sofa while she was helping me clean in the parsonage and didn't seem the least bit interested in learning how to cook? I can say this now, darling, because I am old and have lived life: one should never judge a child because he is naughty and into things. With Button, it seems to me, it was her talent that made her restless. And because she could not stand anything monotonous, she began to live her own life, putting some zip into it, although at times it was the wrong zip. But now I thank God for her and laugh at her lighthearted books and listen to her lecture with confidence and joy.

The story I am thinking of, you and I shared together, and many times afterwards we laughed about it. And Button's eyes, too, twinkle as she recalls the incident. But how could things as complicated as this happen to a normal, upright, pastor's family?

Mama was sitting on the living-room sofa in the parsonage. She felt little and helpless as she watched with tearful eyes while Papa paced back and forth across the large room. His eyebrows were drawn together in a deep frown as though he were fighting a hard battle to control his temper. Their callers, Mr. and Mrs. Emil Roslund, who lived directly across the street from the parsonage, sat in the chairs opposite the sofa and a heavy air of dismay hung over them all.

Mama looked out through the large bay window which faced the Roslunds' similar bay window and her heart ached as she wondered what solution could be found for a problem like this.

"If you will excuse me for a few minutes," Mama said suddenly, "I think I should make us some coffee."

To Mama, coffee seemed to hold a solution for lots of problems. At least it gave her a chance to get away from the room when she just couldn't stand the conversation any more.

It was strange, Mama was thinking. Until a few moments ago everything in the parsonage had been peaceful and contented. Papa had been speaking of how well the children were learning English and how Americanized they all had become. Then the doorbell had rung and the Roslunds had come in and everything had changed. First Mama and Papa had been delighted.

"Come in! Come in!" Papa had greeted. "It isn't often that our good neighbors come to call."

The Roslunds were fine Swedish people even though they didn't belong to Papa's church. They had been a great help and comfort to the Franzons in the first months after they had arrived from Sweden.

For a few minutes they had all just sat and chatted about the neighborhood. Then, like a bomb exploding in the midst of all the friendliness, the Roslunds had explained, "We have come here for a special reason. For the last few weeks we've been troubled, but we didn't want to alarm you. Something strange and mysterious is taking place within these walls." Mrs. Roslund stopped seemingly at a loss for words, and her husband took over.

"I'll come right to the point, Pastor Franzon," he said. "There appears to be a ghost in your parsonage."

Papa and Mama had stared at their neighbors and then Papa had laughed out loud.

"Come now," he said, "don't fool about it. If there's something about us or our parsonage that troubles you, tell us what it is."

"I'm not fooling," insisted Mr. Roslund. "There *is* a ghost here at night when all of your family is out!

We're not fanciful people in any way, but we *have* seen a ghost, or something that looks like one, for three successive Monday nights now."

"You'd better explain that a little more, Mr. Roslund," snapped Papa, who was beginning to lose his usual good-naturedness.

"That's the only way to explain it, Pastor Franzon. There *is* something tall and white and mysterious that floats around in this room on Monday nights."

"And it dances," said Mrs. Roslund. "It dances a weird dance with its arms rising and falling."

"So, it dances too, does it?" said Papa sarcastically. "And it is tall?"

"At least seven feet tall," said Roslund.

"We can see it through this big window because your light is always on, even when you are not in. You'd be surprised how plainly we can see everything through these big bay windows," said his wife.

"I insist that we leave a light in this room," smiled Mama. "I think a parsonage should always have a light shining so that people passing by on the street will think of it as a friendly place."

And it was at that point that Mama had gone out into the kitchen to get the afternoon coffee.

When she came back with the tray, she tried to smile the gloom away. But even the coffee did not seem to help this time. There was an awkward silence and from time to time, Papa glared angrily. Mama's heart was in her throat.

Finally Mr. and Mrs. Roslund got ready to leave.

"We have done our duty, Pastor Franzon," said Mr. Roslund. "I don't blame you for not believing us. I didn't believe my wife when she told me, but then I saw it with my own eyes. I suggest you come over to our place next Monday night and if that phenomenon appears, you can handle it yourself."

"Yes, please come over and call on us. We can watch your living room together then and see what takes place," insisted his wife.

59

"We'll do that," Papa agreed, "but in the meantime, let's not tell anyone. I'm sure there's an explanation for what you have seen."

But after the Roslunds had left, Papa and Mama looked at each other questioningly. Finally, Papa spoke in an angered voice.

"I've had many strange callers, but these beat them all. A ghost! My eyetooth! And right here in the parsonage. America is a strange place to live, but who ever could have thought I would have come to this."

"Oh, Papa *lilla,*" soothed Mama, "don't let's be alarmed or hurt or worried. Let's wait and see what happens next Monday night. Then I'm sure we'll know what to do."

The next Monday night, at the appointed time, Papa and Mama visited the Roslunds. They sat facing their own living-room window, waiting and watching as if the window were a movie screen. Their conversation had gotten off to a very slow start. Papa looked like a thundercloud and Mama knew the Roslunds felt it was better not to say too much until they could prove their accusation.

Suddenly Papa stared at the parsonage window and Mama stood up and clasped her hands. But the Roslunds sat back in their comfortable chairs and relaxed, for this was an old story with them.

Papa and Mama could see very plainly that something at least seven feet tall, white and flimsy, was dancing around in their own proper living room.

"It *is* a ghost, Pontus," whispered Mama, horrified at her own words, "an awful white spook . . . and did you ever see anything that tall? . . . I never would have believed it. You'd better call the police."

"Don't be silly, Maria. There'll be no such call. I don't want this in the newspapers. We must go over there right away. Whatever it is, I'll get to the bottom of it."

Papa and Mama thanked the Roslunds and said

good night, promising to let them know the outcome in the morning. Just now they had to hurry, so the ghost would not get away.

Entering through the back door, Mama and Papa tiptoed into the kitchen and through the back hall. Slowly Papa opened the door to the living room just as the ghost fell into a heap, then suddenly leaped toward the ceiling. It took a moment before the spook realized that it had an audience. Then it stopped and seemed to freeze to the floor by the lamp table. For a moment, it was hard to believe it was not a statue.

Mama looked with wide, unbelieving eyes, and suddenly she turned to Papa.

"That ghost is wearing my new dining-room curtains," she said, and she hung onto Papa's arm as he slowly walked toward the tall, white figure. At first he did not speak, but then his voice rang out through the stillness.

"Whoever you are under that white, you'd better come out quickly."

The ghost came toward them with short, even steps. When it stood directly in front of Papa, a small voice came from under the white. "I am the ghost, Papa."

"Button!" cried Papa and Mama simultaneously. Then the storm broke loose.

"What in the world is the meaning of this?" raged Papa.

"I can explain, Papa," said the voice.

Mama made one clean sweep with her hand and the white material was brushed aside and Papa's high black silk hat, the one he had used for funerals in Sweden, tumbled to the floor. Next came a discarded, tall lampshade from the parsonage attic. Then the white material slid down to the floor and there she stood, the same Button who was always turning the parsonage topsy-turvy. This was evidently her latest adventure. Papa chided himself for not connecting Button with the ghost in the first place.

Button looked ashamed and deflated, but at the same time disappointed and rebellious.

"Yes, it's me, Papa! I can explain it all, but it wouldn't do a bit of good. So I'll just take my punishment and be done with it." Button gave a short sigh. "But this is something I've wanted to be all my life."

"A ghost?" shouted Papa.

"Yes, a ghost if that is what it has to be! But you wouldn't understand in a million years. You never even try to understand!"

"Button, Button," warned Mama in alarm, "don't be disrespectful to your Papa."

"Never mind!" snapped Papa. "I'd better not hear any more. You can explain it to your Mama. After all, those are her dining-room curtains you've ruined. She can punish you. I'm going to bed to think about this and pray for you. I cannot trust myself to be upset any further."

"Yes, Pontus, you go to bed." Mama patted Papa's arm. "But I wouldn't think about it if I were you. You have an important meeting tomorrow and your blood pressure shouldn't go up any higher. I'll handle our Button and perhaps have an explanation for you later."

Papa stalked off up the stairs, looking old and bent and tired. He did not even turn back to say good night. His heavy steps simply died away in the upstairs region of the parsonage.

Button's face relaxed a little after Papa left. "Do you want me to tell you about it from the beginning, Mama?" she asked mechanically.

"Yes, please do, Button," said Mama kindly. "Perhaps that will help us to explain to the Roslunds who have been watching your Monday-night performances from their living-room window."

Button sighed deeply and wiped from her cheeks the stubborn tears she had tried so hard to hold back while Papa was there. Mama would understand how she felt when she knew the story.

"You remember last fall when I asked Papa if I

could enter the talent show the town was giving for young people? I wanted to win the service club's scholarship for the most talented contestant. Of course Papa said no. And the way he said it, I knew the door was closed so tight I couldn't even pry it open. I was broken-hearted because I had written a one-act play that I was going to perform. It was good, Mama! Really good! But I never can do what other girls do because Papa is a minister."

"I know, Button, how hard it is on you. But we can't make your Papa over; you know that."

"Well, I vowed that this year I would enter that contest and that nothing, not even Papa, would stop me. So I decided to enter incognito—and being a ghost was one way that no one would recognize me until it was all over. Then it would have been too late for Papa to stop me."

"Button, that would not have been an honest way to enter, against your Papa's will. How could you have been happy if you had hurt Papa?"

Button stared at Mama. "I guess I just didn't care if I hurt him, I was so mad."

"So this year you were going to be a ghost. But what could a ghost do?"

"I was going to do a very weird dance and call it 'The Lost Ghost.' I found these pieces of material in your sewing room. I thought it was something you had forgotten you had. So I just took it. I'm truly sorry, Mama."

"I'm sorry too, Button. I had just bought that curtain material for the dining room. But I don't think it's spoiled except for those two eye holes you made. I hope I can still use it. Anyway, there's nothing to do about that now."

"After I'd made the costume, or at least learned just how to wrap it around me, I began planning my dance. The only time I could be sure of being alone was on Monday nights when the boys went to the sport club, and the girls to the sewing circle. You and Papa go on social calls that night, too."

"But you have your Missionary-Minded Girls' Guild on Monday nights, dear."

"I stayed until they'd taken the attendance; then I skipped home."

"Oh, Button."

"It worked wonderfully for three weeks. But I was so stupid! I never thought of those neighbors and that bay window with no shade to pull down. I guess I was having too much fun to think. But it's over now. No contest. No prize. No recognition. Papa has won again."

Mama took Button in her arms and kissed her tenderly. "Your punishment will have to be just that—no talent show this fall either. You must learn to bear it bravely and someday you will be grown up and can do what you choose without anyone telling you not to."

"I'm sorry I upset the Roslunds and spoiled the night for Papa and made you sad, Mama. Can I go to bed now? I hope Papa won't be too mad in the morning."

"I think by morning he will have forgotten how he feels tonight. He was insulted when the Roslunds told him there was a ghost in his parsonage. Poor Papa! It isn't always easy to be the pastor of a church."

Watching her daughter go upstairs, looking defeated and unhappy, Mama had a feeling that Button would cry into her pillow tonight. She wished she could help her. She wished with all her heart that Papa was not so strict, but it wasn't within her power to change him. Mama sat on the sofa alone for a long time. She was wracking her brain, trying to find a way to help Button. But Papa had said "no" once before, so that would have to be that. Finally she went upstairs and crept into bed beside Papa. She lay very still, listening for his heavy breathing. But all was quiet beside her, too quiet. Sleep would not come to Mama. Her heart was heavy for Button. That child would do almost anything to try

64

to get what she wanted, and it didn't seem right always to stop her.

Suddenly Papa spoke. "Maria," he said, "can't you sleep?"

"No, darling. I thought you were sleeping though. May I tell you Button's story of why she was a ghost?"

"Yes, Maria, do," said Papa and now his voice was kind.

Mama told him the story and then she kissed him good night.

"Don't worry too much about our Button, Papa *lilla*. She'll turn out all right someday, you just wait and see. She's so like me, Pontus. When she wants something very badly, she just tries to find a way."

The room was still for a long time. Mama thought Papa had finally gone to sleep, but suddenly he spoke again.

"Maria, would you be willing to donate those curtains for a good cause?"

Mama's heart almost stopped for a moment.

"Pontus . . . you mean . . . you think . . . you will let Button be a dancing ghost and enter the show?"

"No, Maria, not in a thousand years would I allow her to enter that show as a foolish ghost-dancer! But there is one way. There is a famous historical poem in Swedish about a ghost. It is called *Vita Frun,* White Lady. I'll translate it into English and let Button act it out in her ghost outfit. After all, the White Lady was a ghost."

"Oh, Pontus! Pontus!" cried Mama with her arms around Papa. "You are wonderful, just wonderful!"

"Now, now Maria," said Papa, "don't think I will give in like this again. But this once I think even God will forgive me if I'm wrong in letting down the parsonage laws. I want Button to know that at times even a Papa can try to understand."

It took Mama a long, long time to go to sleep. She just couldn't wait until morning to see the look on Button's face when she heard the happy news.

Chapter Six

Instead of writing at night, Mama now did her writing to Papa in the morning. It was better that way. When she wrote in the evening, sleep did not come as easily as usual; but in the morning her mind was alert and she did not get into those strange melancholy moods. She wanted this letter to be a happy one right to the end.

This morning the sun was hidden behind a big, gray cloud and it looked like rain, which would be fine for her garden. It was the kind of morning when it would be good to sit down and talk to someone.

Nim had phoned her earlier. He was so thoughtful, that son of hers. Even though his day was extremely busy, he always had time for a few words with his Mama.

"Rest up well now before your trip," Nim had advised. "You're not as young as you were, Mama. And if you store up a little extra strength, it's not going to hurt you."

"I rest every day, Nim. I take good care of your Mama. Don't you think I look pretty good for being eighty-one years old?"

Nim laughed. "I can't see you over the telephone, but I sort of remember that you look pretty good."

It was such a pleasure to talk to Nim. It started the day off right. Soon Emma would call, too. She talked to Mama every day too, telling her to rest, just as Nim did. They all meant so well.

Mama sat down at her desk, her heart light and a smile on her lips, and began to write once more.

Dear Pontus:

In trying to remember just one little detail about each of our children, I've written almost a book.

You were so proud of your sons, Pontus, and I know they were just as proud to have a Papa like you. Pelle, the first sample of our angel model, was so precious as he was growing up, so kind and gentle and thoughtful. He was always ready to help you bear your burdens as a minister and that could often be quite a heavy load.

Pelle has gone beyond all our dreams of his future. His learning has given much to mankind. As an Abbot Professor in a big theological school outside of Boston, Massachusetts, he lives a busy life. God has blessed him in so many ways. He is loved and respected all over the world as a great theologian and has written over two dozen books on religion. We dedicated him to God and he surely has become God's man. Felicia has been the dearest, truest, finest helpmate he could ever have had. She is his right hand at all times and even helps him with his writing. They have one fine son and three lovely daughters, all of whom promise to go far in this world. At times I wish so that you could have stayed on earth just long enough to see how wonderfully well all our children have turned out.

But just now I am remembering a certain chicken dinner we had in our parsonage. You never had an inkling of what a complicated time we had before that dinner finally appeared on the table.

To Papa the ministry involved not only his church duties, but his whole family as well. He wanted his boys and girls to live the gospel which he preached. He wanted them to work with him to make the community aware of the glorious task of the church. If this failed, the ministry had failed. In his heart Papa was sure all his sons would be preachers and both he and Mama would have been thrilled if their girls had all married ministers. The children's religious training began early in life and as they became older, Papa gave them certain projects of importance to perform for him.

One time the project was Farmer Carlson, who lived about two and a half miles outside of Berkley Hills and who was a member of Papa's church in name only. Papa had tried to approach him, but Carlson—having had, with the preacher before Papa, an unpleasant experience which had caused him to stop going to church —would not let any minister or deacon come to talk to him. He had not, however, neglected to give his contribution to the church each year. Because of that and the fact that he had not committed any terrible sin, he could not, according to the church bylaws, be dropped as a member.

For two years Papa had tried to think of a way to make Carlson come at least once to hear him preach, but there seemed to be none. Then one day Pelle offered to try.

"If you wrote him a note," suggested Pelle, "I could deliver it. Perhaps he would consider that, even though he won't talk to you."

Papa looked down at his second son with pride. Pelle was a fine lad and always a joy to the family. He did have a certain way with people and maybe Farmer Carlson would like him. A note might be one way of reaching this stubborn man.

So it was decided that Carlson was to be invited to the important family night at church when a good dinner and a special program were scheduled.

Papa smiled at Pelle's eager face as he gave him the instructions for his call.

"I'll do what you say, Papa. I'll find a way to start

talking to him and then break it to him gently that I am the minister's son and that I have an invitation for him and his family to the important dinner."

"It sounds so easy, Pelle. I'll give you the letter of invitation and I know you can handle the rest.

It was a beautiful fall day. The leaves seemed to be trying to outdo each other in splendor. The sun was still shining warmly, although the calendar showed that it was October. Pelle started out on his bicycle in the early forenoon. He did not know just how he would approach the unfriendly farmer, but he would find a way. He was singing at the top of his lungs, and his feet pedaled as fast as they could.

From the top of a hill he could see the Carlson farm with its sturdy farmhouse and its big barns. There was a large orchard, too. The farmer must be raising a lot of apples. Pelle thought the place looked neat and very friendly.

As he came nearer, he began to feel nervous. Perhaps Mr. Carlson would be provoked and not even listen to his speech. Perhaps he would order him off the property and tell him never to come back. He might even send his dogs after him—that was, if he had dogs. These thoughts were not very pleasant, so Pelle tried to ignore them and think on the positive side. The farmer's wife might be a sweet old lady who liked little boys. She might even ask him in for milk and cookies, and stuff his pockets with apples when he left. His heart was happier already. Anything could happen and he must not build up mountains that were not there.

As Pelle approached the farm, pedaling more slowly, he noticed a flock of chickens by the side of the road. As he came up to them, something, very likely some animal Pelle could not see, scared them and they scattered all over the road in front of his bike. Before he could stop, his front wheel had run over a large speckled rooster. It flapped its wings helplessly and blood spurted out from its neck where the wheel had done its job. Pelle was tenderhearted by nature, and the sight of the wounded rooster brought tears to his eyes. And what should he do now? He couldn't very well come to Farmer Carlson with a half-dead rooster in his hand and say, "Pardon me, Mr. Carlson, but I accidentally ran over your chicken."

No, he had better take the chicken home and ask Mama to doctor it. She could at least bandage its neck and try to make it live. Then he could slip it back among the others and he wouldn't have to explain anything. That would be the right thing to do, for the great cause of Papa's church must not suffer.

Pelle gently placed the rooster in the basket of his bicycle, turned around, and pedaled home faster than he had come. He had a funny, guilty feeling in his heart. Papa would never understand how he could have blundered in his mission in such a way that he had almost killed a chicken, but Mama would. And Papa would very likely be away on his house calls, which gave Pelle some hope.

But when he reached home, Mama was not there. Perhaps she had gone with Papa to visit some old lady who was sick and needed her. The rooster had stopped moving; its eyes were closed, and Pelle could see it was deader than dead. He put it on the table in the back hall and started off toward the church. There was a chance that Mama might have gone there for something and he must tell her of his trouble.

But Mama was not in the church and Papa had just left. The janitor told Pelle a couple of places the pastor had said he would go and Pelle decided to catch up with Papa. Perhaps the right thing would be to tell him the whole story. After all, Papa would know what to do. So Pelle pedaled in the direction in which Papa had gone.

Mama, who had just been to the store, stopped suddenly in the back hall. Someone had brought a chicken to the parsonage. Bless them whoever they were! Just a few moments before she had invited Mrs. Kron over for dinner tonight. Mrs. Kron had been in the store, her eyes red from crying. Only two weeks ago she had buried her beloved husband and she was still in deep grief. Mama had planned to have Swedish meatballs, but a chicken would be so much better.

It was strange that the chicken wasn't plucked, but whoever had brought it might have thought that the folks at the parsonage had more time to pluck a chicken than he did. So Mama sat down and began to pluck out the rooster's many speckled feathers. How good people are to a minister's family, she was thinking, even if they did leave this bird for me to pluck and clean. She had done this many times when they were farmers for two years, so she worked away, singing a song.

God provides in a wonderful way, she thought. Always, when I do a good deed, He is ahead of me with His gift. And her heart was gay and thankful. In an hour the chicken was simmering on the stove. There would be chicken fricassee with dumplings for supper.

Pelle could not find Papa. The janitor seemed to have sent him on a wild-goose chase. When he returned, tired and discouraged, to the parsonage, he was glad to find Mama in the kitchen.

"Home so early, Pelle?" welcomed Mama, smiling. "How did it go with Farmer Carlson?"

Pelle hung his head.

"Before I tell you anything, I have to show you something, Mama," he said as he walked out into the back hall. Then he stopped and stared unbelievingly at the table. It was empty. He drew a sigh of relief. Maybe the chicken hadn't been dead after all. It must have wandered out into the back yard. He must find it at any price and bring it back to Mr. Carlson's flock before he missed it.

"Have you, by any chance, seen a speckled rooster, Mama?" Pelle called into the kitchen.

"I sure have, Pelle. A lovely big rooster with lots of feathers on it. Who brought it?"

"I did," said Pelle.

"You?" questioned Mama. "I thought a farmer member had surprised us with a love gift again."

"Where is it now?" asked Pelle.

"Can't you smell it? It's on the stove. We're going to have it for dinner tonight."

"No, no, Mama! You didn't cook it! You didn't!" cried Pelle.

Mama stared at her young son. Tears were running down his cheeks and he looked as though he didn't have a friend in the whole wide world. She sat down on a kitchen chair and drew him close to her.

"What is all this, dear?" she asked in a gentle voice.

Pelle sobbed out the sad story. And now how could he tell Farmer Carlson that he had killed and stolen the big rooster and his Mama was cooking it and the pastor, whom Farmer Carlson disliked without reason, was going to eat it for supper?

Mama was so stunned that for a moment she could not think. Papa would not be home for a long time and the other children were out playing or working.

"Get Button's bicycle out for me," she said firmly. "You and I must go to see Farmer Carlson right away."

It was a surprised farmer who, with his wife, received a teary-eyed boy and a blushing minister's wife that afternoon. They listened while Mama told how Pelle had wanted to try to get Mr. Carlson back to church and how the devil himself must have been on the job, trying with all his might to stop the boy from doing it. Now, she feared, Mr. Carlson's feelings toward the church would be worse than ever.

The farmer was thoughtful for a long time. Then he winked at his wife and tried hard to keep from laughing.

"How much shall we charge the church for Pelle's

job on my rooster?" he grinned. "What a way for me to get even with all those preachers."

"We are willing to pay," said Mama humbly, "but please don't blame the minister or the church. And I do have one request which might seem bold after all the damage we have done. Would you two be our guests for supper tonight, even though you'll be eating your own chicken?"

"We certainly will!" they both agreed. And Farmer Carlson shook Pelle's hand. "You're a fine lad," he said. "Some other boy would never have told anyone about the accident. I could have just happened to find a run-over chicken dead on the road. It happens quite often. But because of you we will come to dinner and perhaps to that family night, too. I've really wanted an excuse to come back to the church and perhaps this was God's mysterious leading."

It was decided that they should not tell Papa about the rooster. He knew only that his son had done a fine deed, bringing the long-lost farmer back into the fold, and making for the whole family some fine new friends.

It was a happy meal, with Papa telling jokes because he was very pleased. It wasn't often that good works came to pass that quickly.

Chapter Seven

Mama was having breakfast on her porch, facing the garden that looked fresh this morning despite the terrible heat of the previous day. It would be good to leave

Miami now when the days were getting so hot. In a few weeks her garden would look wilted and thirsty as everything else in Florida looked to Mama in the summertime. But this morning there was a tiny breeze coming in from the bay, moving the crowns of the tall palms just a little. Mama suddenly felt sorry for the garden which would have to remain here in the heat without her to love and care for it. How much a part of you a garden could become when you lived with it day after day!

The coffee tasted especially good to Mama, as she enjoyed it with a Danish pastry. She smiled to herself. After she had finished her coffee, she would sit down to write to Papa again. The letter was almost ready now. It was getting very thick with its many, many pages. Today she would write to Pontus about Calle: big, strong, happy, carefree Calle.

It took only a few minutes to do her dishes, make her bed, and pick up the house. Then she was at her desk again and began to write.

Dear Papa:

I have been thinking about our Calle this morning. He was such a good little boy and always stuck up for his Papa. You two were together most of the time when he didn't leave you for a ball game. Yes, Calle was our athlete, a love he has kept all these years. He is over six feet tall now, strong and handsome with broad shoulders. And he has the dearest, tiniest wife! But what a darling she is and just right for him. They have five fine children and Calle holds a position as the head of the Philosophy Department in a large college in Texas. How scattered our dear children are all over this big land!

Yes, Sally and Calle make a fine pair and I am proud of them both. And you should see me with all those grandchildren—two boys and three girls!

It gives me so much joy to have them come for a visit. And when I go there, I can hardly tear myself away, for the children are so dear and lovable. I just melt with so much love and attention.

Being a grandmother is a very precious thing. And now I am a great grandmother also, several times over. Our big family is growing and growing and your name will live on and on through your sons and grandsons. I am so blessed to have seen so many of the coming generation. I am satisfied and happy.

I have loved life and it has been wonderful because it has given me so much that my cup is full and runneth over. The years I have lived in Florida have been restful years and how good that has been for me after all those busy, busy years with a big family growing up, and a Papa in the house who needed so much attention, and all the work in the church. I remember how much commotion there was at times in our parsonage and how sometimes one of the children could change our whole destiny.

Once it was Calle who played the leading role in such a drama. And because, at heart, he had the best intentions there was no punishment in store for him. But I know there was a lot of hurt pride and perhaps a small portion of regret in our Papa's heart.

Both Papa and Mama were very fond of their small church in America. Papa, who was growing old, was sure that Berkley Hills was the last field in which he would work for the Lord and he wanted to be a faithful servant and do his very best.

However, the fame of Papa's silver tongue had reached far and wide among the Swedish-speaking people in New England. One day a pulpit committee from a large church visited Papa's small one. On this particular Sunday morning, Papa outdid himself and

75

preached one of his finest sermons. The committee had been very pleased and moved by Papa's message. They made it clear to him that they were in search of a pastor. And they asked him if he would consider preaching in their church one Sunday morning in the future. Papa promised he would and a date was set for a few weeks later.

"I have no intention of moving from my present church," Papa informed Mama at dinner, as he helped himself to a big spoonful of her Swedish meatballs.

"Then why in the world did you accept the invitation to speak?" Mama asked, looking a bit puzzled.

"Maria," said Papa with authority in his voice, "at my age it would be good for my morale to get a call from a church."

"But you would turn them down, Pontus, wouldn't you?" There was almost a pleading in Mama's soft voice.

"Of course, Maria. Of course," said Papa. "And still, one never knows."

After all, Mama thought, Papa was very human. To be the pastor of a big church in America would make him important in the Conference and there was no doubt in Mama's mind but that he could handle a large membership as well as he had the small one. But if Papa got the call, perhaps temptation would be too much for him and he would say "yes" instead of "no." Mama liked Berkley Hills and she did not want to move away. This game Papa was playing frightened her a little.

Papa looked at the children around the table. A fine crop of children they were and so loyal to him.

"Now, children," he said firmly, "as always, remember not one word to anyone about that church call which might come. You all know that what we talk about inside the parsonage is just family talk, concerning only us. It could so easily be misunderstood."

"We won't tell anyone that we might move, Papa," confirmed Calle.

Papa smiled happily.

"Thank you, Calle. I know you speak for all of my children and that goes for Mama, too." Papa turned to her. "Two weeks from next Sunday I will speak in that church. I'll arrange for Deacon Johnson to take over here; and as that other church is without a minister at present, our church will be glad to share me for a Sunday. Do you and the children want to go with me?"

"I think that would be fun for all of us, Pontus," smiled Mama.

"I think I should say nothing about my family coming along," said Papa. "I'll go in first and you all can come in later and sit toward the back and look around at the church. As I said, one never knows, Maria. Later, when my sermon is over, I'll introduce you to the deacons and perhaps the chairman of the Board of Directors." Papa hesitated for a moment and then smiled broadly at his family. "The committee said there would be an honorarium of twenty-five dollars for my services. Perhaps, Maria, we should be fancy and stop for something to eat in a nice restaurant on the way home. That way you could have a real rest."

The children beamed and Mama seemed very pleased. It wasn't often that Papa could take his family out to eat.

"That would be wonderful, Pontus," said Mama. "But I won't believe you'll really get that money until I see it. Remember that time in Sweden when you were speaking for that big church and thought you were going to get a lot of money. There was that box by the door that had written on it: *For Visiting Ministers.* You dropped in one *krona* and that was all you got, for that was all there was in the box."

Papa looked thoughtful.

"Well, perhaps that served me right. After all, a minister of the gospel should not preach for gain, although it is easy to want money. However, I'm sure the Swedish-American churches have a better system. If they say twenty-five dollars, I think they mean it."

"I hope there's no box by the door," said Calle, looking worried.

"I can assure you, Calle," said Papa, "they will have no box by the door for the visiting ministers. This money is important to me, too, since I've promised to do something nice for my family with most of it."

"Yes, Papa, it's very important for Mama to rest and I hope they won't forget to pay you."

That special Sunday started out just right. Papa was ready early and the children were all excited and very mindful of helping with little things so the family got off promptly. It pleased Papa that he arrived in plenty of time. Mama and the children waited in the car which was parked down the street a bit. When the music from the first hymn swelled out through the church doors, Mama and the children entered. There was only one empty pew at the rear of the sanctuary, so they filed into it and sat down.

It was a beautiful new church. The ceiling was painted blue like the sky and the floor was covered with a thick red carpet. The pews had red velvet cushions, and Papa was sitting on a soft-cushioned chair on the platform. He looked as dear and handsome as ever to Mama. It was hard not to nod at him, but this was an important day, so she would just stay in the background and look around as Papa had asked.

Suddenly Mama was lonesome for their own small, simple church. She felt lost in all this luxury and she hoped the temptation to accept the call would not be too much for Papa. After all, they belonged in Berkley Hills in the church that had been so kind to them when they had arrived from Sweden. It would not be right for them to move from those dear people.

Mama gave each of the children a nickel for the offering as the ushers with white carnations in their buttonholes marched down the aisle. But when the box came to their pew, Mama noticed that Calle did not put

78

his money into it. Instead he stuck it in his mouth. Mama leaned over to scold him.

"Calle," she said, "I gave you that money to give here. How could you do such a thing? Take it out of your mouth right now!"

Mama leaned back against the pew trying not to think about what Calle had done. How could a child of seven get such ideas? Had she not brought them all up to give willingly? She should have made sure that Calle removed the nickel from his mouth, but a solo was being sung and Mama lost herself in its beauty.

Finally Papa was introduced and began to preach. His voice rang out clear and firm and Mama knew he was going to deliver one of his best sermons. But her listening was interrupted by someone choking. She turned to look and there sat Calle, his face getting redder and redder and tears running down his cheeks as he gasped for breath. Mama's heart almost stopped. Calle had not removed that nickel and now he was in real trouble. He coughed a hollow, breathless cough and Mama knew that the nickel must be lodged in his throat. She had to slap him on the back hard, for there was no time to usher him out. It was more important that he shouldn't swallow the nickel. Calle cried out as Mama slapped and the nickel popped out of his mouth and bounced onto the floor. The whole congregation turned around to see where that strange noise was coming from and all the children made little sounds of relief for Calle had looked as though he were breathing his last breath. But Papa preached on through all the noise, even though Calle at one point had almost drowned him out.

Mama had never felt more embarrassed. She was glad the people did not know who she was. She certainly would not wait to be introduced now; she would just take the children back to the car as soon as the service was over. She felt like giving Calle a good spanking for putting the money in his mouth, but it couldn't be done now. He seemed to be his calm self again, and Mama asked him to walk out to the line by the door where Papa stood and say that she and the children would wait in the car until he came. That way, no one would have to know that she belonged to Papa, who must be very angry at the way his family had behaved.

Calle reached Papa after most of the people had left. Only the deacons were standing in a little group talking among themselves. Calle whispered his message to Papa, who nodded as though he were pleased with the way Mama had arranged things.

Just then the head deacon came up to Papa. "That was a fine sermon, Pastor Franzon, one of the best I have heard," he said.

"Thank you." Papa smiled happily.

"But I must apologize to you," the deacon continued. "I don't know where that awful woman in the back pew with all those children came from, but the noise they made was most disturbing. We were most embarrassed."

Calle, who was standing close by, spoke up before Papa had time to answer.

"That woman was Mama," he said softly, "and I made all the noise because I almost swallowed the nickel I was to give in the collection. But it popped out when Mama banged me on the back. Here it is. Please put it in the collection box."

The deacon's face got very red. "I'm so s-sorry," he stammered. "I—I—had no idea it was your family, Pastor Franzon. Accidents can happen to any of us."

Papa's face was grim and Calle wondered why he looked so cross. I'll bet they never paid him the money, he thought.

"Papa," he whispered hoarsely, "did you get it?"

"Did I get what, Calle?" snapped Papa, feeling that Calle had done enough talking for one Sunday.

"The important thing you came for," he said, looking Papa straight in the eye. "Remember that church in Sweden that never paid you for your sermon."

Now it was Papa's turn to have a red face.

"Oh," said the head deacon crisply, "I have your honorarium right here." And he handed Papa the envelope.

"Isn't that good, Papa!" said Calle. "Now we can have dinner out. Won't Mama be glad. This is a good church!"

At that moment Papa could have punished his son openly. But what good would it have done? He thought the deacons acted a little cold when they shook his hand and said good-bye.

Calle ran alongside of Papa to the place where Mama and the rest of the family sat in the car. Papa was so furious that he didn't trust himself to say anything. He just sat down beside Mama and started the car.

"I'll bet you wish you didn't have a family today, Pontus," said Mama sweetly, looking at Papa with wide eyes.

"I guess there will be no call," snapped Papa. "I'm so humiliated that I don't know what to do."

Papa did not say much during the ride home. When they stopped along the way for dinner, everyone was happy except Papa. He knew he had made a terrible blunder in mentioning money in front of the children. But he had learned his lesson, although his pride had taken a deep fall. And he was right about the call. It never came. They must have gotten the wrong impression of his character, and that thought hurt for a long while. But he never punished Calle for the disturbance that Sunday morning; he knew that his son had not meant to do anything wrong, and a family had to stick together in disappointment as well as happiness.

And although Mama never mentioned it, she secretly blessed Calle for his blunder. For now there would be no danger of having to move from the beloved little church in Berkley Hills.

Chapter Eight

Mama wondered why she never seemed to run out of words when she was writing to Papa. There were always new things that came to her mind. She had heard that old people loved to live in the past, and that certainly was true with her. Because life had gone so fast, there were many gold nuggets to go back and pick up. She had the time now to enjoy those little things that had seemed to have very little importance when she was living through them.

She had talked to Vickey over the phone last night. Once in a while the children would call long distance just to talk, as Vickey had. She had been all happiness.

"I was lonesome for your voice, Mama dear," she had said. "John has had four weddings this month and I always get that wedding money, you know. So I'm rich enough to enjoy the luxury of talking with my Mama for a little while."

"Oh, Vickey, how wonderful of you to call! Tell me, how are the children? And how is your John and the church?"

"They're all fine and the church is going as well as ever. I'm so sorry you're not coming to us this summer," said Vickey. "It's really my turn. You've gone to Button so often."

"That's because Berkley Hills is home, little one. Something draws me to it. Perhaps it's all the memories of Papa and my children growing up there. If I'm still here, I'll come to you next summer. That's a promise, Vickey."

"What do you mean, *if* you are still here?" Vickey's voice sounded alarmed.

Mama laughed. "Dear, I have to say that every time I plan something now. I'm getting pretty old, you know, and life is only so long."

After Vickey had hung up, Mama thought perhaps she should not say those things about leaving life. Although it had never bothered her, it seemed to worry the children. But didn't they realize they couldn't keep her forever? But it had been so good of Vickey to call and again Mama marveled at how thoughtful her children were. They were extra special children and she was very blessed, indeed.

Today she would write again to Papa and how she loved doing it! It seemed that writing this letter made her look forward to each new tomorrow. Even the heat did not seem to bother her as it used to. Perhaps this was because she was so happy.

Pontus, my dearest:

Greta was always the "little mama" when she was young. How she mothered her sisters and brothers and how she loved sweets! She was the first "licker." Remember how I called her that because, when I was baking, she would hang around so she could be the first to lick the cake bowl. I can still see her. Her finger went around the bowl so slowly and then right into her little red mouth.

She was a talker, too, and when she went with me to visit people, I had to warn her not to say the first thing that came into her mind. To Greta the whole world was one big happy family and she never thought that anything she said could cause hard feelings. But a minister's family had to be so careful and sometimes we had to handle our members or "would-or-could-be members" with kid gloves.

We never dreamed that our Greta would be the only one of the eight children who would never marry. As a teen-ager and through her college years, she was very popular and never had to sit and wait for dates. But even then her greatest ambition was to study and she wanted to go far in the realm of knowledge. How proud you would be of her, Pontus *lilla,* for she really set education before marriage. And she is very happy and seems to have no regrets now, although I know there was one romance that made a big dent in her heart. There is someone, I'm sure, whom she has never forgotten. Something happened to break up that romance and it has left a scar, but she said very little about it at the time and threw herself completely and wholeheartedly into her studies.

First she became a high-school teacher and now is a professor of foreign languages in a college. These days she is finishing up the work on her doctorate. She has worked about eight years on it and I know she will pass with great triumph and that will be her greatest happiness. She has a cute apartment in Philadelphia, where she has made her home for many, many years. She drives a nice car and takes many trips. There is plenty of opportunity for her to travel, with me living in Florida and the rest of the family all over America. And she has the time, especially in the summer, now that she is through with graduate courses.

Vickey and Greta were always as close as twins, sharing so many things together. Now they are so far apart, too far, I think. Do you know, Pontus, I think it would have been wonderful if all of us could have stayed in Berkley Hills and seen each other almost every day. Why should families have to be separated when they love each other so much?

I shall see Greta this summer, and I am becoming impatient as the time grows near. We can catch up on all the news and I will have so much to think of when I leave. Today I am thinking of when Greta was little back there in our Berkley Hills parsonage.

Mama's greatest delight was company. In Lapland the parsonage had looked almost like a hotel with people coming and going and the many members of the Franzon family. After they had moved to America, Papa was annoyed at times because Mama seemed to overdo it with her many invitations and he craved spells of quietness in which to meditate on his sermons. But that was one thing Mama did not seem to understand, though he had tried to explain it to her many times. Then, too, a big family like theirs was enough to feed, Papa felt, without an extra one dropping in for all kinds of meals.

"Do you always have to have people around, Maria?" he sputtered.

But Mama only laughed at his fussing.

"That is the price you have to pay for having a young wife," she teased. "My home is also for my social life, Pontus! I love giving luncheons and coffee parties and even dinners once in a blue moon."

"Those blue moons come too close together," protested Papa, but he knew it would do no good. The first chance Mama got, she would ask people to come to the parsonage regardless of his feelings against it. So Papa said no more. He didn't want to admit to himself that he was getting older each day, while Mama seemed to stay young and full of energy.

The parsonage in Berkley Hills was very much like the parsonage in Sweden. It was a warm, homey place and the kitchen smelled as a kitchen should, with something good and exciting cooking on the stove or baking in the oven. It was Mama's practice to keep everyone satisfied with plenty of good things to eat. The cooky jar was always filled to the brim and there were extra special surprises on the dinner table when the family least expected them.

Greta came next in line to Mama for enjoying company and she loved to go visiting and to meet new people. Sometimes Mama took her along when she went on special visits for Papa to new families who had recently moved into the neighborhood.

One day, when they had lived in America only one year, Papa asked Mama to make such a call. She was to carry an invitation to some Swedish people to visit Papa's church on Sunday morning and to tell them that the pastor would call very soon. These calls which Mama made were valuable, for she seemed to win people with her friendliness and that made it easy for Papa to move in and do the rest.

On this particular day Mama had taken Greta along and they knocked at the back door as was Mama's custom. When a lady's voice told them to come in, they stepped into a large kitchen. The lady put down the dustpan she was holding, shook hands with Mama and smiled at Greta.

"How nice of you to call," she said after Mama had told of their errand.

They talked for a few minutes and then Greta spoke up, her eyes wide with wonder.

"Mama," she said admiringly, "I think Mrs. Rodstrom is the cleanest lady I have ever seen."

"I'm sure you are right, Greta," said Mama, "but what makes you say such a thing?"

Too late she realized she should not have asked her daughter to explain, for Greta was more than willing to go into detail.

"She's much cleaner than you, Mama. When you sweep our kitchen floor, there's only a little bit of dust in the dustpan. But look at Mrs. Rodstrom's! It's so full it's almost falling over. She must be awfully clean!"

Mama's face fell. Her heart went out to Mrs. Rodstrom, who blushed and stammered a few words about lack of time or something like that. But Mama knew right then that they had failed in their mission to help Papa. Now the only thing she could do was to bake a Swedish coffee ring and bring it to Mrs. Rodstrom the first thing in the morning. Perhaps that would help undo the harm Greta had done with her observations. She hoped with all her heart that *that* would make their neighbor forget Greta's silly remark.

Mama scolded Greta on the way home, explaining that a lot of dirt in the dustpan did not mean a person was very clean. It was really an insult, not a compliment.

Greta was completely deflated. "I'm sorry," she said. "I wanted to say something to make her like us."

Sometime later, on a Sunday night, the family visited a large church in Berkley Hills where all the Swedish churches met for a great alliance meeting. When refreshments were served after the service, Mama noticed that Greta had taken a fancy to a man with a long white beard.

"He looks just like our *Jul Tomten* in Sweden," cried Greta excitedly. "May I go over and say hello to him?"

Mama gave her permission and a little later Greta came over to the table where Mama and Papa were eating.

"I like that man," she said, taking hold of Papa's hand. "Come with me to meet him."

Papa walked along with her against his will, but the man had already seen her efforts, and Papa did not feel he should refuse.

"This is my Papa, Pastor Franzon," smiled Greta.

The man stood up and extended his hand. "I am Pastor Lingren, a retired minister and a bachelor, living at the Y.M.C.A. Glad to meet you and your friendly little daughter. I am originally from Sweden."

Papa shook Pastor Lingren's hand.

"I have already asked him to come to the parsonage for dinner tomorrow night. Is that all right, Papa?" asked Greta proudly.

"I insisted she ask her parents first," said Lingren.

"I am sure you will be very much welcomed," encouraged Papa.

So Pastor Lingren came to the parsonage the next night and it seemed that never before had a guest enjoyed a visit more thoroughly. He was delighted with Mama's fine cooking and he and Papa had a lot to talk about, since both had served churches in Sweden and America.

After that night, Pastor Lingren came to call once a week just about at mealtime, and gradually he increased it to twice a week. But it was the week he came three times that Mama began to worry.

"I don't like it, Pontus," she sighed. "This bachelor pastor seems to take all he can get. I thought twice a week was too much, but now it is three times. We must do something to stop it or he will surely move in as a permanent guest and that I will not have."

Papa stared at Mama. "I can't believe it, Maria! You really have had your fill of company for once. But how can we break off our friendship with this minister so suddenly? He really has nothing to do but to eat."

"Well, he has overstepped his eating with us, Pontus *lilla*," said Mama, "and we have to think of some way of stopping our hospitality without hurting his feelings."

Papa laughed. "You are full of graciousness, my dear. Ideas come easily to you. You will find a way."

But Mama just did not seem to be able to think of one thing.

Late one Saturday afternoon of a week when Pastor Lingren had already had dinner in the parsonage twice, Papa and Mama stood talking in the living room. Suddenly Mama gave a cry of despair. "Oh, Pontus, look! Here comes 'Invite-Himself-for-Dinner' again and of all times, on a busy Saturday afternoon. He's getting impossible. You have to help get rid of him—in a graceful way, of course. How I wish Greta had never invited him in the first place!"

Papa chuckled. "I'd be delighted, Maria, but I don't see what I can do to help you. After all, this is a parsonage and I have to be a gracious host to a brother in the Lord."

"Well, you can try not to talk so freely today, Pontus. In fact, you could even go and make a house call. Invite him to ride along and drop him off at his Y.M.C.A.," suggested Mama, hopefully.

Papa greeted the pastor cordially and soon they were deep in conversation. Papa seemed to have forgotten completely what Mama had asked him to do. She listened at the door from time to time, and it seemed to her that Papa was being more friendly than ever. Yes, Papa must have forgotten and she must remind him in some way.

The children sat waiting in the kitchen for their dinner. Mama looked sullen and, although the table was set and the corned beef simmering on the stove, she made no effort to start serving the meal.

Finally Torkel couldn't keep still any longer. "When do we eat, Mama?" he asked, his mouth watering to taste that corned beef whose delicate fragrance filled the kitchen and drifted into the living room, Mama was sure, right into Pastor Lingren's nostrils.

"Dinner will be late tonight, Torkel. We shall not eat until our caller has left."

"Isn't he going to eat dinner with us?" asked Greta with surprise.

"Not tonight, dear." Mama seemed cross and not at all like their happy Mama.

No one said anything more about dinner and the minutes ticked away on the wall clock. Finally, in desperation, Mama knew she had to do something or she would weaken and let the pastor stay. Then a thought came to her. Why couldn't she write Papa a note? He would be clever enough to use it as an excuse for a sudden call to leave the parsonage and would offer to take Pastor Lingren home. That would be a happy solution to a very knotty problem. She hurriedly wrote a few words on a piece of paper, folded it, and gave it to Greta.

"Give this to Papa, dear," she directed. "It's urgent. See that he reads it right away."

Greta tripped lightly into the living room where Papa and Lingren were discussing how times had changed in the old country.

She made a Swedish curtsy before Pastor Lingren who reached out his hand to greet her.

"Here comes my very best girl," he smiled.

Greta handed Papa the note. "Mama says this is urgent and for you to read it right away," she said importantly.

Papa took the note and turned it over in his hand. "But, Greta, I can't read it without my glasses. Will you get them for me quickly please?"

But before Papa had time to say another thing, Greta snatched the note from his hand. "Pastor Lingren can read it for you, Papa," she said. "He's wearing his glasses. You will read it, won't you, Pastor Lingren?"

"Why, of course! I'll be happy to, my little girl. Here, give me the note and we'll see what it says."

As Greta skipped from the room, Papa had a strange feeling that this was not the way Mama had planned it, but there was nothing he could do now. Pastor Lingren cleared his throat and began to read in a clear, firm voice, which dwindled to a barely audible whisper.

"Pontus *lilla,* get rid of him at any price. Can't you see he's just inviting himself for dinner again?"

Papa was glad Greta had left because a heavy silence had enveloped the living room. Pastor Lingren stood up, stretching himself to his full stature, and put on his overcoat. Then he squared his shoulders and reached out his hand to Papa.

"I'd better be leaving, Pastor Franzon. Give my best

90

regards to Mrs. Franzon and the children. I might not be able to come back for quite a while."

His voice was biting with sarcasm and Papa's voice sounded very humble as he bid the guest good-bye. Was it Papa's strained imagination or did the door shut a bit harder than usual? Mama heard it and came into the living room, her eyes beaming. "Oh, Pontus, it worked, didn't it? And so quickly."

"Yes, Maria," said Papa in a strange voice. "It really worked."

Mama stared at him. He did not seem pleased with the clever way she had gotten rid of their unwelcome caller. There was an awkward silence for a minute and then Papa told Mama what had happened and why Pastor Lingren had departed so quickly.

"That was a terrible blow to the man, Maria, especially coming from you who possess so much charm and graciousness. It was something he never expected, even if he did deserve it. But I must say that, whatever you do, is certainly not done in a small way."

Mama was completely humiliated and tears filled her eyes. To hurt someone was so unlike her kindly way that she could not believe it had really happened right there in their friendly parsonage. Even God must be displeased with her thoughtless action.

It was a good corned-beef dinner, but it was eaten in silence. The children missed Pastor Lingren's happy laughter and funny jokes. They knew something had happened, but did not dare to ask what because Papa's face was so stern and Mama's gay remarks were missing tonight.

Later that evening Mama asked Papa, "Do you think I should go and ask Pastor Lingren to forgive me, Pontus? I could ask him to come back again. I know I would feel so much better inside."

"No! Absolutely no, Maria! What is done is done and your punishment will be to bear it. That man needed to be told and, after all, I think even in a par-

91

sonage you have a right to blow off steam once in a while. Now let this subject be closed forever."

That was the hardest thing for Mama, not to talk about it. For a long, long time the memory pricked like a pin stuck into her loving heart, but she wondered if Papa wasn't secretly glad about it just the same. For now he knew that Mama had found out there can be too much friendliness, even in a parsonage.

Chapter Nine

Mama was writing diligently. Her head was bent over her paper and there was a big smile on her lips. How easy it was to remove herself from the present and go back into the years of long ago. Her hair shone as the sunbeams played on it. Although she was old, only a few strands of hair were really gray. Hers was a happy world and a happy home and writing to Papa made it the happiest of all.

Dear, dear Papa *lilla:*

I think of you so much these days, but they are happy, joyful thoughts. I know that even when people are parted the spirit of the departed loved one is closer than before to the one left behind. The memories you and I share, darling, how sweet they are! Their fragrance is like that of a rose garden to my soul. How can I ever be lonesome when I can dream back like this and when I know that someday I shall fold up my tent-home here on earth, put on my celestial garments, and be by your side for ever and ever?

Only a short time more of this life and I shall have climbed to the top of the mountain. And I'll stand there and shout, "Pontus, I made it! I made it! I made it!"

Death, I am sure, is only a dark tunnel through which we all must pass to get to the other side. It may be dark and damp down in it, but I am sure that a little bit of the glory of heaven will shine through as we look far, far ahead. And that light will guide us safely through until we stand on the shores of eternity and behold a splendor so great that we couldn't even have imagined it. It is God's great, big, loving surprise for us. And I know that you'll be waiting there for your Maria. I get so lonesome for heaven sometimes, Pontus, that I just can't wait until I am called to go.

But sitting here today, I am thinking of Kerstin. She was our baby, the eighth of all the children, such a safe, lucky number. How we loved her, Pontus! And I often wonder if we didn't spoil her just a little bit. It seemed you were never as strict with her as you were with the others. She could wrap you around her little finger.

But she was such a great comfort to me after you had left us. I seemed to be the little one then and she took such good care of me. You see, darling, although I tried to be brave, facing life without you seemed futile. And then as the other children left home for college or marriage or work, I was so glad that we had had that eighth child. She was so happy and full of fun and our home was never empty or lonely. Kerstin dated Konrad for a long time after you were gone. He was a nice boy, but she never loved him. Then one day Mr. Right did come along.

Now she and Jim have been married many years and they have three fine strong sons. Just now Jim is an officer in the United States Air Force, and he, Kerstin and their family are stationed in Labrador. And, darling, our Kerstin is a good wife and a wonderful, sweet mother. She never did grow to be tall like the other children. She's only about five feet two inches tall, and that must be why her four men wait on her hand and foot. But I know that she gives back to them so much love and joy and after all, that is what makes a happy family—this giving and receiving.

You remember, she was always a dreamer; and even when she was a little girl, she was making up songs to sing. Well, she is still writing songs and I know that she hopes, one day, to find that pot of gold at the end of her rainbow and to be as successful as her sister, Button. Pontus, I wish that I could wish on a star for her and see it come true. How very much I want the children to have the things that their souls yearn for! But I am so grateful that she is happy with her handsome Jim.

I have to smile when I think of them. Kerstin followed right in her Mama's steps in one way. She was bound to get Jim, and she did the same thing I did to get you. But let me tell you about her strange romance.

It was such a glorious spring that year. Mama, whose heart had been sad for such a long time since Papa's death, had for the first time begun to feel again that bubbling over joy. Oh, she couldn't help singing and laughing when all the birds in her garden seemed almost ready to burst with their singing just for the joy of living. And so it was with her Kerstin! Kerstin had been walking on clouds since last night when, she claimed, she had met the only one: her dream, her ideal, the man whom she would one day marry.

Yes, last night Kerstin had met Jim.

Kerstin and a girl friend had been to an amusement park. As they stood waiting for the bus that would take them home, they had been caught in a heavy rain storm. Then out of nowhere had come two young men, members of the U.S. Air Force, who put their coats around the girls' shoulders. Soon after, the bus had arrived and they had all boarded it together. Kerstin had invited them all home and Mama, delighted to have company, had made some coffee. After they had left that night, Mama had noticed that Kerstin's eyes were shining like stars.

"I am going to marry him, Mama!" she declared the next morning. "That Jim is my man. He doesn't know it yet, but I do. I felt it the minute we met and oh, Mama, it's wonderful! It lifts you up to the clouds and then suddenly drops you down to this earth again. He is coming back tonight. Just we two are going out. I know he must feel as I do."

Kerstin had talked on and on. Mama had just smiled, thinking that it could be as Kerstin said. Who had the right to interfere with fate? Only the days ahead would tell.

But Mama had only to wait until the following morning to see the depths to which Kerstin's love had reached and to realize the haste with which she had taken things into her own small hands.

It was a starry-eyed young girl who beamed at Mama over the breakfast table. Looking at her, Mama was almost sure that even the stars in all their glory would be outshone by Kerstin's eyes.

"Mama," Kerstin burst out almost before Mama had time to finish the Amen to their morning prayer, "I proposed to Jim last night!"

"You did what?" cried Mama in alarm.

"I proposed to Jim. I thought you did that, too, Mama. Isn't it true what Button told me, that you proposed to Papa?"

"Yes, honey, of course it's true. But *that* was your *Papa!*"

95

Kerstin laughed. "And he was wonderful, Mama. You did the right thing. I know, too, that my Jim will be just as wonderful."

Mama became serious. "Kerstin, your Papa was a minister and don't forget I had been his housekeeper for four years and had known him for five when I told him I wanted to marry him. And besides, he was very, very bashful."

"Well, that's not half as bad as Jim, Mama. He is engaged to another girl!"

Mama stared at Kerstin and her heart began to sink. How could her daughter talk so lightly about trying to take someone else's fiancé? Perhaps she was just joking. But there was no time to find out. Kerstin had kissed Mama hurriedly on the cheek and dashed out the door so she wouldn't be late for work. Mama watched her go and she worried a little.

But that night after they had eaten dinner, Kerstin, still bubbling over with happiness, let Mama share the events of her special evening, relating in detail just what had taken place.

It had been such an enchanting night. When Jim had rung the doorbell, Kerstin had had to hold back her steps so she would not fly to the door. Then she had seen him standing there, tall and dark, smiling at her sweetly enough to make her want to go right into his arms. But she had restrained herself and just let him help her on with her coat. After they had said good night to Mama, they had gone off down the walk and taken a bus to the park. It was too lovely a night to spend at a movie. Kerstin had just wanted to walk and talk and learn to know this wonderful man who seemed to have dropped down right from heaven to her.

Those two hours of walking and talking had been very valuable. They had stopped in at the Lucky Spa for an ice-cream soda and then had come home to sit on the porch in the old hammock which had been used by all her sisters and brothers on dates when it had hung on the parsonage porch. Kerstin, too, had sat with dates in that hammock before, but nothing had ever been like this and nothing would ever be like it again. Jim had been more than she had ever dreamed about, more than she could ever hope to find if she waited from now until eternity. When he had told her that he might have to leave Berkley Hills suddenly, that any time he expected to get secret orders to go somewhere overseas, her heart had begun to rule her mind and she had done nothing to stop it. Jim had held her in his strong arms and there had been a moon, a silly, big, yellow moon beaming down on them from the night sky.

Jim had pressed his cheek against hers. "You are as soft as a little kitten," he had said, caressing her hands. "I wonder though if these little hands have hidden claws."

She had laughed a silvery, happy laugh. "I think they have, Jim; great, big, sharp claws. And they'll scratch anyone who tries to take what I like away from me."

"Oh, that sounds fierce," he had said in a deep voice.

"I might be little," smiled Kerstin, "but I am fierce at times. But you don't have to be afraid. I like you."

"I like you, too."

He had kissed her tenderly.

"Jim," Kerstin had said suddenly, "do you know what? I am going to marry you!"

He had looked surprised and then had laughed heartily.

"No, Kitten," he had said, "you are not. You might as well get that out of your pretty head right now. After all, you just met me last night."

Kerstin pulled herself out of his arms. She looked at him with serious big eyes, softened by the moonlight. "But I am, Jim! I really am! You are *my* man!"

It was then he had opened his wallet and pulled out a snapshot of a lovely, laughing girl with mocking eyes and had handed it to Kerstin.

"This is my girl," said Jim. "We are engaged. As soon as this war is over, we're going to be married."

"But you are not being true to her," Kerstin had protested. "How can you love her and be the way you have been to me tonight? I was sure you liked me."

"Of course I like you, Kitten. I'm crazy about you. But in a day or two I'll be leaving here and I'll never see you again and you'll soon forget about me. We boys in the service have a habit of being nice like this to pretty girls."

That hurt a little at first, and then it was as though her heart could not bear it.

"Jim," said Kerstin, "I'm going to do something I have never done before. Please don't laugh at me because I am dead serious. Jim, I'm going to ask you something and I want you to answer me honestly. Jim, would you like to marry me?"

He looked deep into her eyes and hers never wavered before his look. She tried to read in his what she wanted to see in them, but she could see nothing. They flickered like candlelight in the wind. Then she had heard his voice like a whip cracking over her tender heart.

"No, Kitten, you must understand this. I would not like to marry you."

"That is too bad," she had said stubbornly. "It is too bad, my darling, for one day you will have to eat your own words. This girl, whom you are now so carelessly tossing aside, is going to be your loving wife."

He had laughed at her then, as though she had said something funny, and shortly afterward he had left. Kerstin had stayed there in the hammock and watched him go down the walk and through the gate. He had turned to wave and she had waved back and thrown him a kiss. She listened as his footsteps grew fainter and fainter and until she could hear them no more. Then she had arisen and winked at the moon, giving it one of her sweetest smiles.

"Look after him, Mr. Moon," she had said. "I love that Jim so very, very much and you know he is going to be mine one day. I can wait . . . I can wait . . . I can wait until this war is over."

"That is how I did it, Mama! Wasn't that as good a proposal as any? And you wait and see, when he comes here tonight, he might tell me that he has been thinking it over, just like Papa did. Even he had to take time to think. They all do, I suppose, when a woman pops the question. You just wait, Mama! Soon you will have to plan a wedding for your youngest daughter."

But Kerstin was wrong in her prediction. Jim did not come back that night. Instead, she received a hurried telephone call.

"I'm not really allowed to call anyone, Kitten," he said, "but I did want to tell you that we're off for the unknown. Thanks for everything. Sorry I can't keep our date for tonight."

She had already said good-bye, but still she sat with the telephone in her hand. All the words she had wanted to say to Jim had not come. And when her tongue finally loosened and a torrent of words poured into the phone, he had already hung up.

Mama felt very sorry for Kerstin. In the beginning after Jim had left, Kerstin tried to keep up a happy, brave front. She played with herself a game of being the "gayest of the gay." And each day she waited for a letter, a letter that never came. She had no idea where in this world the man she loved was, but she did know that she loved him and there would be no one else. And so the time passed and then, months later, at Christmastime, there came a short note from Jim, who was in Italy. An APO address was on the envelope and Kerstin sent a New Year's greeting back to him. Another long period of time went by with nothing more from Jim until one day Kerstin came dancing into Mama's kitchen.

"It's beginning to work, Mama," she said, her eyes all aglow. "Jim's girl has married a Marine. Poor dear! His heart is broken and he wants me to be his girl on paper so he can bear his great loss. But it's beginning, Mama! You just wait and see."

Mama saw many things those days, for on the spur of the moment Kerstin joined the Waves, hoping to be sent overseas where Jim was. But she never got any nearer than Washington, D.C.

Not much later, the war ended and the boys began coming home. Jim would be out in a few weeks, but Kerstin still had another six months to serve.

It was then that the miracle happened. The letter Kerstin had been dreaming of came as a tiny note stuck in a lovely pocketbook Jim had sent as a gift from Italy.

Will you marry me, Kitten, as soon as I get home? I think you were right in the first place. I love that little kitten with the hidden claws. As soon as I land, we'll be together for always.

Kerstin did marry her Jim as he had finally asked her to. Then it was he who had to wait until she was free from the service.

Mama moved to Florida just after Kerstin's wedding and waited eagerly for them to come for a visit.

When the time finally came and they took their belated honeymoon, Mama thought she had never seen so much happiness wrapped up in two people. There was no doubt in her heart but that her youngest, who had followed her way and proposed to her man, had done the right thing and would live happily ever after.

Mama smiled as she folded her letter. How strange the way things repeated themselves! She herself had never regretted having popped the question to Papa that day so long ago, and she was sure Kerstin would never be sorry either. She and Jim belonged together.

A man, thought Mama, is a strange combination of too many wills ruling him at the same time. Sometimes a woman just has to take over and lead him like a lamb to the altar because that is the only way he'll ever get there. Mama smiled at her thoughts. Papa would not have liked being referred to as a lamb, and Mama had a feeling that Jim wouldn't either.

She put her letter away and stepped out of her dream world to busy herself around the house with many things.

Chapter Ten

Dearest Papa:

My letter is drawing to a close. It seems as though I have lived almost a whole lifetime over again. It has been so wonderful and I am glad I have written to you. In a couple of days I shall leave this little home and travel North. I shall fly and enjoy all the comforts of our modern age. I think you would have loved flying, Pontus *lilla;* it takes you places so quickly. All is in order here. I have wrapped and tucked away little gifts for each one of the children to find when they come here. You see, darling, I know I shall not return. It is such a strong feeling I have in my heart. But I don't feel sad. It is as though you look at a keepsake that someone very dear gave to you and suddenly you decide to put it away. So you wrap it tenderly and put it aside. This is what I'm doing with my little home. I have loved it so much and

I've loved life. But, Pontus, this thought has come to me: If life can be so beautiful, how much more beautiful must be this thing called death. Surely God would not have created us to die and be lost in nothingness. No, a wonderful new dimension must be waiting for me and I am sure you and I will dwell there together for ever and ever. In a very few days I shall lock the door to this little white bungalow and leave it with a blessing and a smile. I know you would want me to be this way and I would like to be what you wanted me to be.

Today I am sitting here with an old journal. The pages are so yellow and brittle I can hardly turn them for fear they will fall apart. I call it *The Parsonage Journal* because I wrote in it when I first came to work for you. I wrote in it because I had to tell someone how I felt, and I couldn't go around telling your church members that I was going to marry their pastor. So I talked on paper. And I have saved the record all these years. I have read it through these last few nights, reliving those uncertain days when I told my heart I could not fail, that I would win your love. Let me read aloud a few pages as though I were reading them to you. This first one is so precious:

Pastor Franzon's Parsonage: Lapland, Sweden, 1898
I am here! I have been here just a short time! I am the maid now, but soon I shall be the Mrs. Of course, the pastor has no inkling of that. If he had, I would go out on my ear. But this dear old parsonage knows it, for I am telling it the news every day. And each day I kneel by the big double bed in the pastor's bedroom and pray that soon I will be the wife who will share this lovely room with him. It puzzles me why, if he had decided to be a bachelor all his life, he furnished the bedroom with a double bed? There are many mysteries that surround my preacher, but I shall solve them one by one.

I am beginning to know what food he likes and dis-

102

likes, how hot he likes the house, when he wants me to be gay and sing and laugh and when he wants me quiet. I dress as neatly as I can. I wear lovely, frilly aprons. I see that a little curl always falls down on my forehead and that there is a tiny one at the nape of my neck, but as yet I don't think he has noticed. Last night I studied my face in the mirror and it pleased me. My eyes were big and blue and my hair was a mass of curls.

He had looked at me so strangely during supper. (When we don't have company, I'm allowed to eat with him. He says I'm good company.) Well, last night he kept looking at me from time to time and then down at the corner of the table that wasn't covered by the cloth. I had a feeling he was conscious of how lovely I looked and wanted to tell me so, but he didn't know how. Just as I had finished the dishes, he called me into the living room and told me he had something important to tell me.

"Maria," he said kindly, "I want you to come with me into the dining room."

The sunset was beautiful from the dining-room window. I thought perhaps he wanted to stand in front of it so he would have a good setting for our little tête-à-tête. Then he took my hand, something he had never done before. My heart melted and there were butterflies in my stomach. But still it was a beauitful feeling. I didn't say it, but I knew something was going to happen in those few minutes.

And it did! The old silly, instead of taking me to the window, led me to the dining-room table and there he let go of my hand.

"Maria," he said briskly, "as we were eating tonight I discovered some scratches on this beautiful mahogany table. Will you please tell me how they got there?"

I was furious. I had to get hold of my temper which was beginning to soar. I steadied my voice as I said I was sorry, but I had not noticed them before. I looked closely at the table so he wouldn't see the tears begin to gather in my eyes.

103

"Pastor Franzon," I said softly and properly, as a maid should, "Friday night the treasurer brought in the change from the collection at that special Thursday meeting and just as I came into the room I saw him pull the cloth to one side and dump the money on the table so you could help him count it. 'I don't want to dirty that fine cloth,' he said and grinned at me. But, by then, it was too late to tell him that the table was more important than the cloth, for the damage had been done."

Pastor Frazon looked down at me then and there was admiration in his eyes.

"I never even thought of that, Maria. You are a wonder for such a young girl."

And that was it! What can you do with a man like that! And all the time I thought it was me he was looking at. Oh well, I have just begun my war and I shall win it, though it looks as if it might take a long time.

I wrote daily after that. You did not get any more romantic. Every time I thought I had you, you eluded me in your very matter-of-fact way. But I didn't let myself get discouraged, for I had fallen in love with you, not because you were a pastor, but because you were you.

A year later, I wrote this in the *Journal:*

Today I really did it! I don't know if he will ever forgive me, but I'm glad I did it! And when I become mistress of this parsonage, I shall do it every time we have a party!

The pastor was entertaining the church board at dinner. Of course, the farmer members donated chickens, potatoes, milk, and cream in such quantities that Pastor Franzon did not lose a solitary cent by giving the customary once-a-year party. And I, Maria, did all the work and the cooking and the serving. But the table looked bare to me with the lovely china, the glassware, and the brightly shining silver and only one lone geranium in the middle of it. It didn't look right. So I took seventy-five öre from the housekeeping money and bought some cut flowers. I didn't ask him if I could because I was afraid he might say no. Because they were for the parsonage, the lady at the florist shop gave me a big bunch of roses, and how they dressed up the table! I think he should have been proud and happy; but just before the guests arrived, after taking a last look in the dining room, he came out into my kitchen where I was pouring some heavy cream into the chicken gravy.

"Maria," he demanded, "why didn't you tell me who brought me the flowers?"

I smiled my sweetest smile. "Because I did," I said happily. "I took seventy-five öre out of the housekeeping money because I wanted the table to have a festive look."

He stared at me with eyes that could have burned right through me and then he really laid down the law. Coming from a minister of the Gospel, I could hardly believe my ears!

"Maria, this is my parsonage. If I want you to buy flowers, with my money, I will tell you to. You have overstepped your authority as a maid and to teach you a lesson, I shall deduct that money from your salary this month!"

And with that, he left the kitchen, the mean old skinflint! The nerve of him! To stoop so low as to take it from my meager salary. I'm supposed to count working for him as serving the Lord, but I'm sure even the Lord does not want me to work this cheaply. I feel like giving him my notice. But I can't. How can I, when I love him? And that I do.

But believe me, when I become his wife, lots of things are going to happen that he never dreams of now. So I will swallow my pride this time and let him permit me to give him the flowers, but I will get even with him someday.

Yes, darling, you were all confused in those

days. How much you needed me to set you straight! And I must have loved you a lot or I would have left you. After all, I didn't need to work as a maid. I could have done many other things, but this was the only way I could think of to catch you.

Two more years passed. I knew I had become part of your parsonage in such a way that it would be very hard for me ever to leave it. And I knew that you had wonderful qualities, too, but it seemed I only wrote in the *Journal* when I sputtered about something. But here, I've come across a few sweet lines:

The parsonage garden is so beautiful. Some men from the church come to work here and they do a wonderful job. They love their pastor very much and so do I. I love to see him come up that walk, so straight and strong, with that look of anticipation in his eyes as though he couldn't wait to open the door.

I can see it coming along slowly, this love I am waiting for. He is more gentle with me and at times when we plan meals and things about the house, I know he almost forgets I am the maid, now graduated to housekeeper (with five whole kroner added to my salary each month). At Christmastime he gave me a lovely Bible inscribed: "May God bless you, Maria," and he signed it, not Pastor, but Pontus Franzon. All these things are a sign that soon now he will ask me to become his wife.

I laugh when I look at him sometimes and say to myself, "You don't know that you are going to be the Papa of many children and that we all are going to live this parsonage to pieces." There are so many things he doesn't know, especially about me kneeling beside his bed each day, praying over and over again, "Dear God, give me Pastor Franzon for my husband." But I can wait a little longer, yet in my heart I pray it will not take too long for that handsome bachelor pastor to make up his mind.

I have an entry in the journal after I had told you I was going to leave for America, hoping against hope that you would tell me I needn't go, that you wanted me with you always. But you didn't. I was brokenhearted when I had to leave, but I never showed it. I acted as though going to America was my heart's desire. But, oh, how I missed you and how I wondered about you and the parsonage! I wrote this when I had been in America only two weeks:

I can't believe it, but I did leave Pontus. And even though my heart broke into a thousand pieces, he did not know it. Before I left, I cooked up lots of food for him and wrote little notes telling him where to find things. I had been a part of that parsonage for four years and lately he had left most housekeeping decisions to me.

When I was on the big Swedish-American Liner, I was so lonesome for the parsonage I could hardly stand it. I wondered if the plants were being watered and if they were getting enough sun, and if the lilacs were in bloom in the garden and if Pontus was still taking his long walks. I wondered if he remembered to lie down an hour before dinner so his nervous stomach would not kick up and give him trouble. Every room came into sight in my imagination, every nook and corner. I longed more than ever just to see dear Pontus coming up the walk and to hear his voice calling my name.

But here I am in a strange big country and I am going to write him a letter soon and give him my address. It could be that Pontus, too, is lonely and perhaps he will ask me to come back and marry him. It could be. But I must wait again, wait to see if he answers.

I was so happy when your letter came, but so terribly disappointed when I read it. You wanted me back all right, but only as your maid. I wrote you then and gave you my terms. I was so far away that I didn't care what you thought of my offer to be your wife. You did not write again and knowing you so well I had had a feeling you wouldn't, for love had not yet awakened you. Then one summer day that we could never forget I saw you on a bench in Central Park with the sun shining on your golden hair. My heart almost stopped beating, and I knew that life would never seem right if you and I did not travel the road together. We finally did come to terms, even if circumstances almost stopped us from getting married. I gave my notice, giving up my good salary and my job as second cook to a wealthy family. But I would have given up a gold mine for you, darling. We took that leap into matrimony at last—a frightening one for you, but I pledged my life to make you happy.

And so, I wrote one last time in my beloved *Journal* only a few hours before we sailed on that big boat back to Sweden and our parsonage.

I am married to Pontus! It is a miracle, but it is true! I am so happy that it hurts inside. What a strange life we have started together! I must remember to go slowly. My darling is so bashful. I must remember to think before I talk. Pontus has to get used to my being his wife and not his maid. But the first day in our home I shall kneel again by that big double bed and say a prayer: "Thank you, dear Lord, thank you with all my heart for giving me Pastor Franzon for my husband. I promise to love him through joy and sorrow forever."

In an hour he will be here to get me. My heart is beating so fast it almost frightens me. I wonder if he will take me in his arms like other bridegrooms. I pray that he will! He is so strange. If he doesn't, I must not fret, but be willing to wait. At last my beautiful dream has come true.

So farewell, dear *Journal*, I shall always keep you because the precious story of my love is on your pages. You know I never wanted anyone but my Pontus. And may God add His blessing to our lives.

That was the last thing I wrote, Pontus. I never opened the *Journal* after that, but kept it as my dearest keepsake. Now I shall part with it. I shall put it in the fireplace in my garden and set a match to it, for no one else shall ever read it. This story belongs only to your heart and mine.

It is getting late, darling, and my eyes can hardly stay open. I am finishing my letter to you. But I shall see you soon, so this is a happy "so long," my darling.

Always yours in life and death,
Maria

Mama pressed the letter to her lips and placed it in an envelope which she would give to Emma. On it she wrote, "To Button."

Her heart felt light as though she had just fulfilled a mission. Now she could give herself to other things. Tomorrow she would have a long visit with Emma in her lovely home. She would spend most of the day there and take the letter to her to keep.

The last day before her trip Maria would be with Nim and Karin. Of course, Nim would not be at home until dinnertime, but she and Karin would have a good visit until he joined them. Then would come the last morning when her pleasant journey would begin.

Chapter Eleven

It had been such a wonderful party! Mama was still basking in the glow of it when she awoke that last morning and hurried from bed to make herself ready. Today she was leaving. How sweet it had been of Karin to invite so many of her friends to the chicken barbecue last night. Somehow it had taken the sting out of parting.

Mama knelt by the sofa in the living room for her morning prayers and as always she mentioned each of her children by name, asking God to care for them on this special day. But Mama went further than her own family. As she lost herself in meditation and worship, her prayer of love covered the whole world and all its people not forgetting the sad, or the lonely, or those who had no one to pray for them. The living room was bathed in sunlight as she arose from her knees. It was going to be a beautiful day for flying. Emma had said that she would be at the airport to see her off. Mama smiled to herself as she sat in her kitchen having coffee. How lucky she was to have so many people who loved her. If she was mistaken, if she did return from her trip this summer, she would have so much to come back to.

Now everything was in order. She would strip her bed and Karin had promised to see that the sheets and towels were laundered and put back in the linen closet. Mama took one last walk in the garden, snipping off a couple of flowers to take with her. And then she said good-bye to it.

"Bloom and bloom, little flowers," she whispered.

"And, grass, do the best you can in the hot summer. Mr. Gale will water you and love you. But no one can love you as much as I have."

Mama had always talked to her garden and her house plants. "They love it," she told her friends. "Just try it on yours and see how they thrive."

When Nim drove up, she was waiting for him.

"As soon as I get you settled in the car and put your suitcases in the trunk, I'll come back and see that the door is locked," said Nim.

"No, Nim dear," answered Mama sweetly. "You just put the suitcases in the car. Don't think I'm being silly, but I'd like to lock the door myself."

Nim frowned a little. Why did Mama talk so strangely and why did she have an almost mysterious look on her face as though she were up to something? But he did not say anything, just busied himself with the suitcases as Mama lingered behind.

"Good-bye, little home," said Mama. "Thank you for being so happy and dear." And a tear came despite Mama's trying to hold it back. She felt so unusually emotional today. It must be because of the letter to Pontus, she thought. He would tell me that I'm beginning to dramatize my own thoughts. She was laughing as she approached the car where Nim stood by the door, waiting to help her in. Karin smiled at her from the front seat and Mama winked back.

"I'm getting to be a selfish old woman, children," she said. "I don't even trust Nim to see that my house is locked when I leave. Why don't you scold me?"

"Mama," said Karin, "you're just your old sentimental self. There isn't a streak of mistrust in you."

"Thank you, Karin. Now I can fly away in peace. But you're right. I just wanted to be the last one out of my house and to say good-bye to it."

There was so much to talk about on the way to the airport, so many greetings for Nim and Karin to send along to the dear ones in the North, that in no time they were there.

Emma greeted them in the lobby and squeezed Mama's arm. "You have a beautiful day for flying, Maria. God be with you till we meet again."

"And you, too, Emma. Take care of yourself and look in on my house once in a while. Thank you for taking care of my plants. You're about the dearest friend I could ever have had."

It had been easy to say good-bye with all of them smiling so happily. Mama had waved to them from the round window in the airplane and they waved back. Soon the plane started up and in a moment she was high up in the clouds, heading for Rochester, New York. It was a long flight and she had to make three changes. But the day went in a calm, easy way, although she realized that she was tired. There had been so much excitement and perhaps she had worked herself up a little with her thoughts of not returning. After all, life was not in her hands. She must not think about that any more. Her thoughts and heart must be with Torkel and Nancy and their two fine sons, Ben who was a college freshman, and Mark, a senior in high school. It would be so good to be with them and get to know them again. She had seen them only for brief periods when they made their visits to Miami.

It was dusk as the plane landed in Rochester and Mama could see Torkel standing there waiting. Her heart gave a quick beat. How much like his father he was. It was as though the years had been rolled back and her own Pontus stood there in the twilight waiting for her. But soon she was in Torkel's arms.

"Welcome, welcome, Mama!" he greeted her. "Nancy is home making sure that dinner will be on the table when we arrive and the boys are helping her. But I know you can see through that. I really wanted to have you all to myself for this short time going home from the airport."

"You have a new car, Torkel!" exclaimed Mama excitedly as they got into a new Chevrolet.

"Yes, Mama. I wanted it now so we could have fun taking little trips. We're so happy that you are going to be with us almost a month before you leave for Button's."

"It will be fun," whispered Mama, stroking Torkel's arm. She was glad to sit back in the comfortable new car. She felt very, very tired, which wasn't at all like her, just at the moment when she should be the most excited. It must be because of all that changing of planes. The trip had seemed so long. She guessed she was old now and couldn't travel as well as she used to. But she would have a restful night and soon she would feel like herself again.

It was a precious month of June for Mama. Torkel spent all the time he could with her, and Nancy waited on her hand and foot. What a lovely, beautiful person Nancy was, she thought. And even the boys took turns helping and entertaining Mama in every way. But at night, when the boys had gone out, Nancy would sit down at the piano and Torkel would take out the old, worn, Swedish hymnal that had once had its place in Papa's church in Lapland and they would sing, the three of them, in Swedish, all the old loved hymns that meant so much to Mama. Even Nancy sang in Swedish, coached by her husband. She had learned a little of the language when they had spent a couple of months in Sweden while Torkel was doing some research for a degree.

Mama loved those nights and the time passed quickly. Then one day there came a letter from Chicago, from Pelle who was teaching at a conference there!

I will be driving by in a few days, Mama, so why don't I take you to Button's? It will mean that you have to cut short your visit with Torkel, but it will work out so well and be so much fun. And we will be able to stop in and say hello to Torkel and Nancy, too.

Torkel promised not to fuss if Mama left a little earlier than planned. They had had such perfect weeks together and it would be good for Mama to be taken right to Button's doorstep.

Mama telephoned Button who was delighted.

"I can't wait to see you, Mama," she said. "It's been a long, long time. I have your visit here all planned. We'll have a big party with all your old friends, and take trips, and do everything your heart desires."

"Thank you, darling," Mama answered Button's stream of words. "It will be so wonderful. Only your Mama is a little tired, so don't invite any people until I've been there a few days. I need to rest first so I will feel like my old self again."

"Mama"—Button's voice was troubled—"there's nothing wrong, is there?"

"Of course not, little one. Oh, how sorry I am that I frightened you. I'm tired, that's all. After all, Button, I am eighty-one years old."

There were only two days left to be in Rochester. Mama and Torkel had so much to talk about and did it mostly over cups of coffee while Nancy tactfully busied herself doing other things. Mama and Torkel could tread ground where Nancy had never been, recalling times when Papa had been with them in Berkley Hills and Torkel had been doing a lot of growing up.

One afternoon Nancy had gone to the hairdresser and the boys, too, were out somewhere. Torkel had had to do some calling for his church and Mama had had a few hours alone. For the first time in her life she felt an uneasiness she could not explain.

If only Torkel would come soon, she thought to herself. I'm lonesome, really lonesome. I used to welcome being alone, but I seem to dread it today. I feel that for some reason Torkel should be here with me. These are the last days we'll have together, for I'm too old to travel any more. I can never make a long trip like this again.

114

When the front door opened and Torkel's happy hello rang out, Mama's heart was glad. All was well now. Her boy was home and they were together again.

"How about some coffee, Mama?" asked Torkel, wiping his forehead.

"It would taste good, son. You know your mama and her afternoon coffee."

"Come on in the kitchen, Mama, and talk to me while I put the coffee on. I'll start peeling the potatoes for supper, too. Nancy will be glad to have it done when she comes back."

"You're a fine boy, Torkel, a fine son and a thoughtful loving husband. I'm so happy for you and Nancy and your boys and your wonderful church. These Sundays when I have listened to you preach have been a little bit of heaven for me. God is good to have given me such wonderful children, and I'm so grateful."

"Yes, my church is growing. We have new members and the church has increased its giving to the Lord's work. I'm happy here and so grateful to have my little Mama with me to share my joy."

Torkel poured the coffee and set out some fresh raised doughnuts which he had just bought.

Mama was delighted. "You know how I love newly baked things, Torkel. Thank you for bringing the doughnuts."

"I love them too, Mama," laughed Torkel. "I love them and I shouldn't. I'll have to cut out these fancy in-between meals after you leave. It isn't good for my waistline."

Mama laughed. "To me your waistline is just right, Torkel. You look just like your Papa."

"I'd like to be like him in every way, Mama. I'm working on it. And like my Mama, too! You've taught me so many things I'll never forget. I want you to know how much your love means to me."

It was quiet in the kitchen. The clock on the wall

115

ticked loudly and the summer wind blew the curtains a little. Torkel, leaving his seat to lower the window a little, waited for Mama's sweet voice, but no words came. There was only a heavy silence. He turned back to the table and suddenly the world seemed to have come to an end. Mama's head was resting on her bosom. There was a strange twist to her mouth, her blue eyes were closed, and she had lost consciousness. Torkel rushed to her side. He had seen seizures like this before among his parishioners. He knew Mama had suffered a stroke—his dear, lovely Mama—and there wasn't a thing he could do for her except to call a doctor. Carefully he carried her seemingly lifeless light body to her bed. He had never realized until now how little Mama had become in the years since her heart attack.

By the time Nancy returned, the doctor was standing over Mama. On his orders, she was rushed to the hospital and Torkel started to notify his brothers and sisters. He tried to keep his telegrams from being too grim, to break the news in a gentle way. Meanwhile, Mama was resting in the hospital and the doctor had not yet been able to give a verdict.

The days which followed were dark ones. Mama regained consciousness, but she had lost her voice and her right side was paralyzed. She didn't seem to be in any pain, only confused, and it seemed hard for her to understand what had happened to her.

"I don't think she will ever know what happened to her," said the doctor. "Part of her brain is damaged, due to the shock, and she can't remember anything of the past. She only knows what's happening now."

Button and Eric were the first to reply to Torkel's telegram.

"We're coming right away," said Button over the telephone. "We're leaving the first thing tomorrow morning and we'll drive as fast as the law allows. She'll be well again, Torkel. I know she will. Let's all pray as hard as we can."

116

Torkel repeated Button's words to Nancy.

"It will be so hard on all of you, darling," she said with tears in her eyes. "But I don't think Mama would want us to pray too hard for her recovery. Let's pray easy and leave it to God. That is what Mama would tell us."

Torkel kissed Nancy gently, knowing she was right. They must not despair and storm the gates of heaven for Mama's recovery. God had the span of her years in his book of life. To "pray easy" would not be to try to hold Mama by force, but to let her slip away gently if that was God's will.

Chapter Twelve

Button was sitting beside Mama's bed in the hospital, with Eric standing beside her. Both of them looked tenderly down at Mama lying there so little and white. This was the same Mama who had declared some years ago to Nim that she would go to heaven anytime, but never to the hospital. Perhaps now even she knew that this was the best place for her.

Nim, who had been in touch with Torkel every day since Mama's stroke, was flying up from Miami the next morning. The other children were standing by, waiting to hear if Mama's condition should take a turn for the worse. If so, they would be ready to come immediately.

It had been a sad meeting when Torkel had greeted Button and Eric on the steps of his parsonage.

Button had thrown herself into his arms. "Oh, Torkel, it can't be! It can't be! Mama must get well and come to us. Don't you think God will let her come this one last time?"

"Button is very upset, Torkel," said Eric. "She's almost ready to break. She's been counting the days until Mama's arrival."

But sitting beside Mama, Button became calm. Mama looked happy. Her eyes were big and blue and full of love and joy as Button kissed her on the cheek. She knew Mama couldn't talk, so she had said very little, thinking it might be difficult for Mama not to be able to answer. Mama had patted her with her left hand as if to say, "Don't worry, little one, I'm happy. They're all so good to me."

And the nurses were good to Mama. They seemed to want to linger by her bedside.

"She's a dear," one nurse told Button. "Even for a glass of water, she reaches up her well hand and pats your cheek. She's sweetness itself."

"She was always like that," answered Button. "She loves everyone. She will bless each little task you do and pray for you, even if she can't talk."

"I hope she'll recover," said the nurse. "A person like that has so much to give to this cold world of ours."

"She will be well," said Button. "She will want to come home with me. Mama can will herself to do anything. Soon she will be up walking and talking."

Eric had left the room and returned with a beautiful bouquet of cut flowers. When Mama saw them, tears came to her eyes and she patted his arm.

"I know how much you love flowers, Mama," he said simply.

Button stayed with Mama until late that night. It was as though she could not tear herself away. And in the morning she was right back there, sitting on the same chair, holding Mama's hand and smiling, although her heart was breaking. At times she would close the door

118

to the corridor and sing softly one of Mama's favorite Swedish hymns:

Snart randas en dag så härlig for mig
och all som älska Gud
där sol ej går ned på levnadens stig
och aldrig hörs klagans ljud.

Mama would smile and try to join in. And although she could form no words, a little bit of melody came through.

When Nim arrived, Mama looked at him strangely for a moment and Button, reading her thoughts, felt sure that Mama knew Nim would not leave Miami and all his patients unless her illness were serious. They talked very little. There was not much to say. Button did not want to hear a doctor's view of Mama's illness. She felt she must cling to the hope that Mama would get well, and she would believe it regardless what Nim or any other doctor might say.

"We will see that she gets therapy for her speech," said Nim to the nurse. "We will do all that can be done for her."

Nim had given many orders and talked with the doctors. Mama had looked so happy while he was there. But when Nim bid her good-bye, tears ran freely down her cheeks and she tried to hold on to him. Nim cried, too, though it was not like him to cry. It frightened Button and she looked helplessly at Eric who put his arm around her.

"Don't forget, dear," he said kindly, "Nim is not the doctor right now. He is a son who has to travel far, far away from his Mama."

That helped Button a lot. Eric could always say the right words.

The evening after Nim had flown back to Miami, Eric left for Berkley Hills, but Button stayed on.

"I'll stay until Mama is better," she told Eric. "You understand."

So Eric drove home alone. Button knew he was worried about her, but he couldn't take the pain from her heart. How blessed she was that she lived near enough to Torkel to come and be with Mama. Each one of the children would be happy to be in her place. The waiting must be terrible for them.

The days passed slowly. Torkel and Button spent most of their time in the hospital and Mama was getting better. One day the nurse had wheeled her out to the sun porch and Mama had watched a gray squirrel hop from tree to tree and a young mother with her baby. It was good for Mama to see people and trees and cars again. Soon the therapy would begin. Button had tried to teach her how to form some words and had succeeded in getting her to say, "I d..o..n'..t kn..o..w." It was a wonderful accomplishment and Mama said it over and over, Button was sure, just to make her daughter happy. Yes, Mama was better. God would let them keep her at least a short while longer. And so Button decided to go home for a few days.

She said to Torkel, "If Mama gets worse in any way, let me know immediately and I'll fly right back."

Torkel promised and Button knew he would look after Mama as well as she could, for he was just as anxious for her recovery.

"I'll leave tomorrow morning, Torkel, right after breakfast. Perhaps I should see Mama first, but right after we visit her, you can drive me to the airport."

Together they spent the evening with Mama. She seemed very happy and much stronger. She moved her sick hand just a little, as though she wanted to tell them: "See, I can move it a little. Soon I will be able to move it more."

They had such a happy time in the hospital room. Mama was so gay and sweet and when the time came to part, Torkel and Button stood on each side of the bed. "We shall pray, Mama, before we leave you," said Torkel.

Mama nodded her head. She was pleased.

They placed their arms around her and repeated together a little Swedish prayer Mama had taught them as children.

> *Gud som haver barnen kär*
> *se till mig som liten är*
> *vart jag mig i värden vänder*
> *står min lycka i Guds händer*
> *Lyckan kommer*
> *Lyckan går*
> *Den Gud älskar*
> *Lyckan får.*   *Amen.*

They kissed Mama and she smiled up at them.

"Sleep, darling. Close your eyes. I'll come to see you in the morning before I go home. You're so well that I can leave you now," Button whispered, patting Mama's cheek.

Mama closed her eyes but opened them again quickly. Button closed them gently with her fingers. *"Sov gott, Mama lilla,"* she said in Swedish.

Mama's eyes were closed when Button left the room, hurrying down the corridor to catch up with Torkel who had gone on ahead.

The next morning Button was up bright and early. Her suitcase was packed and all was in order for her leaving. She was having breakfast with Torkel and Nancy in their sunny kitchen when the telephone rang shrilly, echoing through the house. Torkel went to answer it. Nancy and Button were laughing gaily when he returned and stood in the doorway, making no attempt to rejoin them at the table. Both Nancy and Button stared at him.

"Mama has left us," he said. The words came slowly as if each one were a great weight and tears rolled down his cheeks.

"No, Torkel! No! No! Tell me it isn't so! It isn't! It . . ."

Both Nancy and Torkel comforted Button and they all comforted each other.

"She slipped away during the early morning hours," Torkel said after they had calmed down a little. "The nurse said she found her gone."

"But she was so well last night, Torkel, the best she had been," sobbed Button.

"Mama always wanted to die well," said Nancy soberly. "Don't you remember how she used to say she couldn't see why one should die sick when one could die well by just closing her eyes on earth and waking up in heaven?"

Nancy was right! This was God's way of taking Mama home. Perhaps that was why she had been so happy last night. Perhaps Mama had known in her heart and the shining in her eyes had been the joy of heaven. During the night she had taken the fastest turnpike there was, traveling with lightning speed, up, up, up, and now she was there. Mama had stepped out of her sick, tired body as easily as one stepped out of a dress. She had left it behind and her real self was perhaps singing with the angels at that very moment.

There was so much to do that morning that Button stayed. Helping to break the news to all the sisters and brothers was hard, the hardest thing she had ever done. But Torkel was strong and tender and so kind as he took over all the arrangements. Mama was going home to Berkley Hills after all, but this time to be buried there from the little church she loved so much.

All the children came home for Mama's funeral, and all eight of them stayed in Button's home. They walked quietly and spoke gently through the ordeal of meeting people in the room full of flowers among which Mama rested. It was a beautiful July day when they laid Mama to rest where the tall pines guarded the peaceful cemetery. The service was beautiful and never could a pastor have given a more glorious message of life which could never die. A friend of Mama's sang her beloved Swedish hymn:

> He the pearly gates shall open
> So that I may enter in . . .

The feeling of the people had been one of triumph. It was like saying good-bye to a dear one who had started a long journey. The pastor's talk gave Mama's children hope and courage.

Many friends followed to the cemetery, standing silently, more in awe than in sorrow, as the last words were uttered and the abundance of flowers placed on the black dirt. Upon invitation, all went to Eric and Button's home where Button had arranged a lovely coffee table in the old Swedish tradition, just the way Mama would have wanted it. It was such a help to have so many kind friends close by during those first hours after the final good-bye to Mama.

Presently they were alone—Mama's eight children, some with their husbands or wives and children. Dinner had been prepared by kind friends who had seen that everything necessary for the meal had been brought to the house. It was good for them all to be together for a little while. They talked very little of Mama, for their hurt was still too great. But each of them tried not to look sad. Mama wouldn't have wanted that.

"It is glory," she would have said, "no sadness, just glory. You can all walk alone now. I was with you a long, long time."

They all could feel her dear presence in their midst. And after another day and night, the time came to part. It was harder than usual this time because Mama had always held them together. She had been the one who had relayed news from one to the other.

"We must write," said Greta. "I promise to write to one of you each week until I have gone all around the seven and then I'll start all over again."

"Yes, we must not lose touch," said Calle.

"Let's have a reunion in Miami soon and you all can come to visit Karin and me," suggested Nim.

"Or to us in Minneapolis! Minnesota is so much like Sweden," put in Vickey.

"Yes, we must be sure not to forget each other. We must write and tell each other little things, just like Mama did," came from Torkel.

"The best way to honor her memory is to pray for each other as she did for us," said Pelle. "I'll miss most of all her prayers of love and protection." And they all agreed that that was really Mama's way.

"I think you're all so wonderful," said Kerstin, the baby of the family. "I wish we could stay together for a long time. It will be hard to go back to Labrador when my heart is so close to all of you. I just can't think how it will be not to get letters from Mama each week. Please write to me, all of you."

"And I," said Button, "have been the luckiest of all to have you here in our home. I know I speak for Eric, too. I feel especially blessed because I can go and put flowers on Mama's grave and kneel there to pray when I get too lonesome for her."

So they had left, one by one, with hugs and promises and tears mingled in among the good-byes. But each had to go his own way. They were Mama's children, taking up Mama's mantle, trying to be a little more like her each day. Because what she had planted in their hearts had begun to bear fruit in abundance, each felt, stronger than ever, the need to be true to their very best and to give of themselves to others. Such was the seed Mama had sown.

Her children had called her blessed and now it was their turn to live so that their children could draw from this source of strength. And because of all Mama had taught and done in love, the dreams of truth and right and beauty which she had created within their hearts neither sorrow nor death could destroy.

Epilogue

The mailman arrived at Button and Eric's cozy home with a big Manila envelope. Button's name was written on it clearly in big, even letters. It had come from Miami and in the upper left-hand corner was Emma Ostrom's address. Button hugged it to her heart. What could dear Emma, Mama's wonderful friend, have sent her? Perhaps it was something which had belonged to Mama. Emma knew how sad her heart was and wanted to cheer her up. It was such a thick envelope. Button sat down on the porch in Eric's favorite chair and pulled out the sheets of paper. But it wasn't Emma's writing at all! It was Mama's! Tears filled Button's eyes and her throat felt dry as she thought of dear, sweet, beautiful Mama. She found a little note attached to the top sheet. It read:

Button, dearest:
  Your Mama asked me to mail this to you if she did not return to Miami. Here it is. I will write you a long letter later when your heart is not so sorrowful.

Love,
Emma

Then, with a fast-beating heart, Button began to read Mama's letter to Papa.

That was a strange day. Mama was gone and yet, Mama was right there beside her. She read at intervals all day, doing only the necessary things in her household. At night she still had a few pages left, so she took them to bed with her. She hadn't told Eric about it yet, but he was so used to her reading things, he had asked no questions. After she finished the letter, she lay very still for a long time. Eric slept soundly beside her.

"Mama," she whispered, "I'll try not to be sad, but to know that you are happy, so very, very happy. I know I mustn't wish you were back. I must bless your memory and let you go." Then closing her eyes, she drifted into sleep.

Button awoke suddenly and then, in the twinkling of an eye, she knew she had been dreaming. But she was glad she had dreamed, for it had taken that sharp edge from the pain she had had in her heart since that morning in Torkel's home when the telephone message had come that Mama had left this earth. The dream had been a very comforting one. It was as though Mama had been trying to say in her sweet, calm voice, "Don't grieve, little one. I'm so happy here, happier than I ever was in earth life."

In her dream Button had been sitting on a beach by the seashore. It could have been Miami Beach where she and Mama had spent so much time together, but she had had no clear knowledge of where she was. She knew only that the ocean was calm and that a hot afternoon was slowly melting into evening and the big, red sun was sinking into the blue-gray water. No painting could ever have produced the brilliance of those colors playing on the western sky. She was hugging that glorious picture to her heart when suddenly she saw a tiny white boat gliding along with the outgoing tide. It seemed to have appeared out of nowhere, and it was not very far from shore. Someone stood up in the boat and waved to her, and Button's eyes had been wide with joy and wonder. It was Mama! She wanted to rush

126

to her and hold her fast so she would never leave her again, but the water between them was too deep. So Button called out, making her voice loud and strong, "Mama! Mama, come back! Please, darling, come back to me!"

And Mama had smiled. It had seemed so good to Button to see again that dear smile she had known so well. But then Mama shook her head and her blue eyes looked tenderly toward the shore.

"No, no, dear, you must not call me back. There is no way for me to come back. This boat has no oars and no motor. It is going to glide right into the sunset and I am going with it to the land of eternity. Don't look sad, little one. Be glad for me because this is such a wonderful journey."

Then, as Button watched, the little boat became smaller and smaller as it glided farther and farther away from shore until all she could see was a tiny speck way out on the endless blue. And soon, a rose-colored cloud enveloped the little white boat and it was gone and Button could see it no more.

She knew she must have been crying in her sleep because her cheeks were wet and there were tears in her eyes. The dream had been so real and Mama had been so gloriously beautiful. Button would have been happy to keep on dreaming, but now she was back to life again, a life without Mama.

It was very early morning. The first rays of light played on the curtains. Through the open window, fresh pure air drifted in. Outside in the big oak tree, the birds were twittering to each other. Everything promised a beautiful new day. For a while, Button's mind was busy thinking about her dream, living it over and over. Then slowly she slid out of bed, very quietly, so she would not awaken Eric. She tiptoed through the hall into the living room and flung open the front door to welcome in his majesty, the sun, who was rising in the East in great splendor. It was a beautiful sunrise!

And somewhere in that beautiful eternity was Mama.

Somewhere she was smiling her warm, sweet smile as lovely as the sunrise. Mama had finished her journey on earth, had reached her goal and had entered triumphantly into the greater life, still a mystery to those left behind. But to Mama, it was a reality.

It must be wonderful, Button was thinking, to look forward to eternity as Mama had done, to meet the last moments of life with calm anticipation. Mama's faith had held to the end and left a strong rock for her children to stand on.

Button heard Eric moving about in the bedroom. He would be wondering where she was. Then she heard his footsteps coming down the hall in search of her.

"Button," he called, "where are you at this time of the morning?"

"Here I am, Eric," she called back to him, "here on the front steps, drinking in the beauty of the new day."

In a moment he would be beside her, his hair standing up in all directions, his bathrobe on crooked, and his eyes still drowsy with sleep. Dear Eric, she still had him and love and home and children and grandchildren. Life was still so rich and blessed. And the children of Mama and Papa, all eight of them, had promised to keep in touch and never lose contact with each other. Mama would be so pleased.

Love had been Mama's key to life. Love had moved mountains for Mama and in love her children would live their lives. For a mother like Mama could never die. She would always be a living presence.